KD GRADE 5 Megan Graff $1.00

The Pony Vacation

is

Awesome

Gill Morrell

The Pony Vacation

ISBN 82-591-1146-2

To David, Andrew, Fiona, and Richard

Chapter 1

I sat on the edge of the bed and shivered. Outside, the sun sparkled on the stream that bordered the fields. If only, I thought, if only it would start raining.

I looked at the two empty beds. I made my own bed slowly, tucking in the sheet and arranging the duvet carefully over the pillow. But maybe it'd be better to leave the bed untidy. Maybe that way I'd be told to tidy up after breakfast.

I ruffled the sheet hastily, scrunched the duvet in a heap on the floor, and threw the pillow on top of it.

"Jess! Breakfast!"

"Coming," I called, stuffing my pajamas under the bed to add to the untidy effect.

"It'll get cold!"

In the big dining room, all the others were already sitting around the long table. There was the sound of cheerful conversation. Someone laughed. They were so confident and happy, all looking forward to another long day out on their ponies.

All, that is, except me.

"There you are at last. Sit down here and have some cereal." Mrs. Butler was warm and cozy and motherly. She patted the empty chair next to her, and I slipped into it gratefully. I looked at the plateful of corn flakes in front of me and felt my tummy turning somersaults. I rubbed my arms and asked for orange juice.

"Here you are, dear," said Mrs. Butler. "Get on now, or you'll be late. Would you like a boiled egg after that?"

"No thanks," I mumbled. Delaying tactics were one thing, feeding eggs to a stomach full of butterflies was another. I dawdled over my cereal as long as I dared. Good, everyone else was finishing and getting up. Now Mr. Butler came in and looked straight at me.

"Get a move on," he said, not unkindly. "Can't be late your first day, can you? We'll be ready to set off in a minute."

"Oh, but I haven't tidied my room yet. It's an awful mess," I said.

But Mr. Butler just laughed. "This isn't a boarding school. You're on vacation. No one minds a little mess, and you're the one who'll have to sleep in it! Come on, the others are nearly ready."

Reluctantly, I got up. It was no good — there was no way out. I was going to have to do it.

*

Six weeks earlier, my favorite dream seemed to be coming true.

"Please don't go home and say you *have to* go on the trip," my tutor, Mrs. Angatell, warned us. "But it's a great opportunity. Some of my class went last year, and they had a fantastic time."

I'd rushed home, thrilled. The leaflet promised everything I wanted most.

Farm Pony Trekking
Mr. and Mrs. D. Butler offer places for young riders
of all standards for weeklong vacations in beautiful
unspoiled countryside. Great food and comfortable
farmhouse accommodation.
Long, exciting treks on your own pony each day.

It went on to detail the exact costs and where the farm was.

I burst into the kitchen. Mom was feeding one of the twins and the other was sitting in her high chair, banging the table with a rattle and making ear–splitting screeches.

"Mom, Mom, look at this! Can I go, please Mom? Please say I can!"

Mom looped some stray hair behind an ear and looked up wearily. The twin being fed, Tim, spat out his mouthful of soft, mashed vegetables. Then he picked up the mess with his fingers and stuffed it all back into his mouth again. I shuddered in disgust. Meanwhile, Holly sent up an angry cry.

"Give us a moment, Jess," said Mom. "Sit down and help with the babies a minute. I'll have a good look at whatever it is after they've finished."

Everything's always after the twins have been sorted out, I thought crossly, slinging my bag on the table. I perched on a stool in front of the two highchairs with their forest of metal legs and picked up the bowl of baby slime. It was going to be a revolting job.

I filled a spoon and put it into Tim's half–open mouth while he was still busy gazing at me. He swallowed obediently. Quick as a flash, I repeated the action for Holly and, while she was swallowing, Tim got his next mouthful. I felt a real glow of pride as the level in the bowl dropped. I scraped the last spoonful off and waved it between the babies. It was funny watching them both reaching eager arms to get it. I pushed it into Tim's mouth. Tim's better than Holly. They're both noisy and smelly and keep the whole family awake at nights, but Tim's livelier and funnier. You'd never know they're twins except that they're the same age. Tim's fair and dimpled with bright blue eyes. Holly's much darker. What hair she has is black, her eyes are greenish–brown, and her skin looks tanned, though they

were only born at the end of last summer. People say she looks very like her big sister: Me.

Mom looked exhausted — she was always energetic and enthusiastic before the babies came. We used to spend loads of time together in the evenings and during the holidays, and she always had time to help me with homework. Now, even though she doesn't work at the library any more, Mom never seems to have a spare minute. It's not really her fault, I know, but it's hard not to blame her sometimes. Dad does his best to make up for it, but he's out at work till late each evening. And the twins take up the weekends.

"OK, then, let's have a look," said Mom. I pushed the leaflet across the table. I watched Mom reading, though out of the corner of one eye I could see Holly squishing banana up her nose.

"Well, I can see why you want to go," said Mom at last, "but I don't see how we could possibly afford it."

"'It's an especially good price, Mom, it says so."

"Sorry, love, it's just one of those things."

"Oh, Mom, please!" I pleaded. "Couldn't I get a job – a paper route or something?"

"Come on, love, you're not even 14 yet. I'll mention it to your Dad, but he'll say no. Everything's so expensive these days..."

I stormed up to my bedroom and slammed the door.

Predictably, when Dad came home, he took one look at the advertisement and said, "Sorry, Jess, not a chance. We might manage a week away during summer, in a camper by the sea or something, but not this. Maybe another year." He turned away to give Tim a cuddle.

I was furious. In another year, there'd be all sorts of other expenses. Anyway, I wanted to go now, not next year. This year, next year, sometime, never — always an excuse I thought bitterly.

9

"Everyone else'll be going!" I shouted. "They all said they'd go home and get their parents to say yes. You're the only really mean ones – it's not fair. It's all your fault – you and the horrible twins!"

I ran upstairs, crashing my door shut again and waking the babies.

"Jess! You behave!" shouted Mom angrily as she came upstairs to sort them out.

I didn't answer. I just crawled under the duvet and reread the leaflet. "Long exciting treks... beautiful unspoiled countryside... your own pony..." It was just too good to be true. I'd read so many books about riding. I'd spent so many hours daydreaming about galloping through woods or jumping huge fences or just looking after my own pony. Sometimes he'd be a delicate palomino. Other times, he'd be glossy black, fiery and brave, or a sturdy New Forest gray, or a chestnut thoroughbred. It didn't really matter what I dreamed; I knew I'd never have a pony of my own, not where we lived – not even if we lived in the country. And riding lessons cost the earth. But this trek – all my friends would be going, and I couldn't see why I shouldn't be able to go too.

At school next morning, I kept to myself. All the gossipy, friendly huddles were sure to be talking about the pony trek. I'd be the only one left out.

In math class, Mrs. Angatell was wandering around looking at our work. I hadn't done much.

"Something the matter, Jess?" she asked.

"No, miss," I answered automatically.

"No problems at home? Those twins of yours all right?"

"They're OK."

"And you're feeling all right? You're not ill?"

"I'm fine!" I insisted. Mrs. Angatell sighed and picked up the math book, almost as if she didn't want to.

Then at lunchtime my best friend Martha kept asking if I

was ill. I wasn't going to explain. I found a corner outside where I could sit and dream in peace. The rough asphalt tickled the backs of my legs, and I wondered what it would feel like to jog along on a pony through the heather, or to canter over wide grassy hills with the wind in my hair.

I'd been too angry and disappointed to go to sleep easily last night. Now, in this sheltered corner warmed by the spring sun, my eyes closed, and I dozed, wavering in and out of pony dreams.

Mrs. Angatell's voice broke in oddly. For a moment, I couldn't remember where I was, and clutched at imaginary reins.

"Jess, whatever's the matter?" Mrs. Angatell was saying. "This isn't like you. You'd better come inside, and I'll phone your mother."

Dazed, I let myself to be escorted into the little sick room. I could hear Mrs. Angatell in the office next door, phoning home.

"Your mother will be here to get you soon, and I'll ask Martha to stay with you till then," she said afterwards. "You should've said you don't feel well."

"I'm all right," I insisted, but Mrs. Angatell just smiled and shook her head and went back to lessons.

There was a knock at the door. Martha put her head round. She was twiddling with her hair extensions, like she always does when she's worried about something – it drives her Mom crazy.

"You OK?" she asked.

"You don't have to stay. I'm not ill."

"I'm not going back to history if I don't have to." Martha squirmed onto the edge of the windowsill and watched me till I couldn't stand it any longer.

"How many are going, then?" I said.

"What?"

11

"You know, on the trek. How many people brought their forms back today?"

Martha looked puzzled. "No one, I don't think. Why?"

"Well, you're going, aren't you?"

"Me? You must be joking. I don't think Mom'd let me, but I didn't even ask."

"But we're always planning to go pony trekking. Don't you *want* to go?"

"Not a chance," said Martha, shaking her head emphatically. "Talking's one thing, doing's another. You'd never get me near a real pony."

I could hardly believe my ears.

"Well, have you heard who else is going? I've kept away from everyone today; I didn't want to hear them all talking about it."

"What are you upset about?" said Martha. "You know what happens – we get one of those letters and everyone talks about doing whatever it is, but no one really does. It was the same with that football tour last term. The boys all talked, but none of them really wanted to go." She stared at me. "You don't mean you really do want to go, really and truly, even on your own?"

"I'd give anything to. But I won't. Dad's too mean. He won't let me. It's all because of the babies. Mom and Dad don't care about me now. Ever since the babies were born, nothing's been the same."

"D'you think they'd have let you go before the twins?"

"How do I know?" I felt confused and angry. "All right, maybe they wouldn't have – but at least there wouldn't have been the twins in the way, using up all the money. Mom's always so tired now. She never has time for me." I could hear my voice getting whiny. I knew what I was saying was unfair. So what? Everyone was unfair to me. I stared at Martha defiantly.

Just then the door opened and Mom came in. She looked concerned.

"Oh, Jess," she said, "what's the matter? Come on, I'll take you home."

I felt silly, but also angry, and I certainly wasn't going to fall on Mom's shoulder for a good cry, which is what I really wanted to do.

"Come on, love," Mom said. "I've left the twins with Anna next door. They'll be all right for a bit. Let's go for a walk."

It was really odd being in the park on a school day. There was hardly anyone about and the ducks all came waddling over at top speed in case there was any bread going.

Mom and me walked along without talking. Mom felt for my hand. I nearly didn't let her hold it, but then I thought I would. I'd forgotten how nice it is to walk along hand in hand. Mom always has to hold the stroller now, or the shopping bags, or, worst of all, she carries one of the babies.

We sat on a bench by the edge of the lake. I nibbled at a rough fingernail. Now Mom was being so nice, I felt mean, but I still wanted to go on the trip.

"It's that pony trek idea, isn't it?" Mom said. "Do you want to go away that badly? Dad and I didn't realize."

I didn't say anything.

"Well, maybe Dad and I could find the money from somewhere. We'd not be able to go away in the summer, though."

I looked at Mom's tired, pale face. I felt guilty, and yet a part of me still wouldn't let go and give up the idea of the trek.

Mom tried again. "You know it's hard while the babies are little. It won't be so bad when they're older and more fun."

"Oh, Mom, I'm sorry," I said suddenly. "I do like having the twins – well, some of the time I do. It's just, when I remember how it used to be, just you and me and Dad, and all the fun we used to have."

13

"But don't you remember how much you used to moan about being an only child? That's partly why we decided to have another."

"I never said I wanted two!"

I could see Mom trying not to laugh. "Come off it, Jess. It's not exactly a choice, you know that. It's a matter of luck – we just happened to get two. And they're really not so bad. Tim nearly said "Jess" today, you know."

"Did he?" I asked eagerly. "Are you sure?"

"Sure," said Mom. "You should see their faces light up when they hear the door key when you get home from school. It's the best part of their day."

"It doesn't really make any difference to the pony trekking, though, does it?" I said, bitterly. "There's not enough money to let me go, not unless you give up your vacation. I'm not mean enough to ask for that."

Mom patted my knee. "I know you're not," she said. "Let's go home now and see what the twins have been up to. Then we'll put our heads together to think about what can be done. Maybe we could manage a riding lesson or two during the summer holidays."

At our neighbor's, Holly was singing tunelessly as she shredded the newspaper. Tim was on the sofa, fast asleep. His fair hair rested damply on his forehead. Holly looked up and gurgled, "Jeh, Jeh, Jeh." I picked her up and cuddled her. Ink–blackened fingers squeezed my neck affectionately. She smelled warm and sweet, almost biscuity, and clung to me. Forget ponies, I thought suddenly.

Mom thanked Anna and picked up Tim, all floppy, and we went home.

I tried very hard to forget about the pony trekking vacation after that. Mom didn't say anything more about it, and Dad gave me some extra pocket money and more hugs than usual. School carried on as normal. No one mentioned the holiday. Like Martha said, no one had taken the advertisement seriously.

Then one evening, we were watching television. Mom was sticky from spooning chocolate pudding into Tim, who kept drooling it out of the sides of his mouth. Holly had discovered that banging a spoon makes a really good noise. It's not easy to enjoy the twins when they're like that.

The announcer read out the week's Lottery numbers. Mom said, "Jot them down, Jess, there's a love. Dad's got our numbers – not that we ever win anything." So I found an old envelope and scribbled the numbers down and that was that.

Mom looked extra tired, so I put the twins to bed. Tim was a real pain. He soaked me with bath water and wriggled non-stop, and Holly filled her diaper as I put her in her crib so I had to start all over again.

Dad didn't look at the numbers for ages, but when he did he got really excited. He phoned to find out how much he'd won. You wouldn't believe how quickly my imagination pictured a new life with loads of money and holidays abroad and a swish car and, best of all, my own pony. But, of course, it wasn't like that.

"Well, Jess, you're in luck!" was the first thing he said when he put down the phone.

"Have you won the jackpot? Are we going to be rich?"

Dad laughed. "No, love, not rich, but it's a nice little amount. Enough to buy a few bits and pieces around the house and maybe a better holiday than we'd planned – and, if Mom agrees, I think we can afford for you to go on that pony holiday, if you'd still like to?"

Chapter 2

The next few days were filled with planning and packing as the Easter holidays had nearly come. The farm people sent a letter explaining how to get there and the clothes I'd need.

"If jodhpurs and riding boots are not available," it said, "other trousers and rain boots may be worn. Jeans are definitely not advised in case of getting wet."

"I don't suppose I could have proper riding clothes?" I asked tentatively.

Mom laughed. "No, love. We need to use this windfall very carefully and there's no spare for extra luxuries. But we'll buy you a pair of leggings down at the department store, and they'll be a bit like jodhpurs. It'll have be that and jeans for dry days."

I worried that everyone else would have proper riding clothes and would laugh at me, but there wasn't anything I could do about it, and it seemed ungrateful to make a fuss. I worried because there was a rule that you couldn't phone home except in emergencies; even cell phones had to be handed in, not that I have one anyway. The idea was that people would get more homesick if they're allowed to phone. I worried, too, if everyone else would already be with a friend and I'd get left out. And I was worried because I was going to arrive late; the only way I could get to the farm was by long-distance coach, and there wasn't one on the first day, which was a Sunday, so I wouldn't arrive till Monday afternoon.

The whole family came to the bus station to see me off, even Dad who took an hour off work. It was the first time I'd traveled any distance alone, and I felt very grown up as I put my bag on the rack over a window seat. Mom and Dad each held a twin, and they all waved like mad. I brushed a few tears away with my sleeve and told myself fiercely not to be a wimp.

The journey went on forever. I was so bored by the time the coach finally reached the town nearest the farm, and I felt sick, even though it was hours since I'd eaten my packed lunch. A tall man wearing riding boots and jodhpurs was waiting for me.

"Jessica Price?" he asked cheerfully. "Hi, I'm Dave Butler. We'll be back just in time for iced tea and you can meet the others. They've had a good first day's ride, up onto the moors. Off we go, then."

"Isn't anyone else arriving today?" I asked nervously.

"No, they all came yesterday. You're the last."

"Can they all ride?"

"More or less," said Mr. Butler. "You're a beginner, aren't you? You'll get the hang of it soon."

Mr. Butler swung the car through narrow country lanes. Primroses starred the hedges and the air was clean and sweet. I sat next to him, my hands clenched into tight fists in my lap. In all the time I'd been imagining the holiday, the one thing I'd never considered was that I might be the only beginner. I had only the vaguest idea, based on books, of how to ride. What if I made a complete fool of myself? Would they all laugh? Would they expect me to gallop and jump fences right away?

At last we reached a lovely old stone farmhouse. Daffodils and tulips were crammed together in the

17

flowerbeds under the front windows. Voices floated through the soft air. Someone laughed.

Mr. Butler got out and stretched. "Get your bag from the back, Jessica, and I'll introduce you."

We met Mrs. Butler in the wide entrance hall. She seemed nice, but very busy. "You're Jessica, aren't you?" she said. "You'll be sleeping in the room opposite the top of the stairs. You're sharing, of course. Now, let's see..." She consulted a list and pushed me through a door.

"This is the common room," she explained. "Everyone, this is Jessica, she's just arrived. She's sharing with Rosie and Kate. Show her where to go and everything, will you dears?"

She patted my arm and then she was gone. I looked back, but there was no sign of Mr. Butler either. I turned back to the room and blinked. There seemed to be dozens of faces, all staring at me. The noise of conversation had died away and only the theme of "The Simpsons" television show filled the silence. Then a tall, thin, pretty girl, who looked about a year older than me, detached herself from the crowd.

"Hi, I'm Kate," she said. "You're sharing with me and Rosie, my sister. She'll be along in a minute – she's still tangled up with a hoof pick!"

I smiled doubtfully, wondering what you do with a hoof pick. Kate took me by the arm and led me around the room, telling me names, but I hardly took in a thing, except that absolutely everyone was wearing proper jodhpurs, and they all seemed totally confident. After a bit, I found myself squashed at the end of a battered sofa next to Kate. Conversations whirled all around me, but I was part of none of them. In desperation, I glued my eyes to the television to look busy, but really I was listening to the ebb and flow of talk.

"... he just can't get the stride right," one girl was saying. "Every time we do a combination fence he goes wrong."

"My teacher always puts a grass rein on them," someone else said.

"... and, of course, I fell straight off in the mud."

"... but we had a cool gallop on the downs. We only stopped when we got to a five-barred gate. I thought Mystery was going to jump it."

"... and she didn't even know what a snaffle was for!"

I shrunk back into the sofa and tried to make myself very small. What on earth was I doing here? Jumping? Galloping? Falling off? Well, I thought grimly, I'll be doing a fair bit of that. My eyes fixed firmly to the TV screen, I tried to remember all the things I'd learned from books about ponies and riding, but my brain was a complete blur.

"Come on, it's supper." Kate was pulling at my arm impatiently. Everyone had already left the room. They'll think I'm a total idiot, I thought.

I slipped into the most inconspicuous place possible at the long table and kept my head down. There was pizza with chips and salad followed by doughnuts oozing with jam and fruit, and mugs of hot chocolate – and I was hungrier than I'd thought. I was crunching into an apple when an argument started between two boys at the other end of the table.

The taller one, whose black hair framed a very pale face, said scornfully, "You're just a pathetic show-off."

"Oh yeah? How come I've been doing jumping for the last year, then?" answered the smaller boy. His fair hair and piercingly blue eyes reminded me heart-wrenchingly of Tim at home.

"That's what you say. You're just a big talker. I bet you've never ridden anything bigger than a Shetland before this week. How old are you, anyway – 8 years old?"

The smaller boy flushed red and pushed his floppy hair back from his face angrily. "I'm nearly 13, not that it's any of your business. I'm not very tall, but that doesn't matter. I can ride anything you ask me to. Anything." He looked around defiantly. Everyone had stopped talking and was watching. The other boy laughed.

"OK, we'll give you a chance to prove it."

"When?"

"You'll see."

There was an unmistakable note of menace in the air. No one seemed to breathe. Then Mrs. Butler came in, and everyone relaxed and started talking normally. Everyone, that is, except me. I stayed quiet and still, watching and listening, more nervous than ever.

There was a video after that and then Mrs. Butler shooed us off to bed.

"You've had a long day, all of you," she said, "and it'll be longer tomorrow. Get plenty of rest. We don't want anyone falling off his or her pony from exhaustion tomorrow."

Kate showed me to the bedroom. It was plainly furnished with three single beds and a wardrobe and chest of drawers for us to share. Rosie was already there, and I recognized her from suppertime. She was short and plump with ginger hair and freckles. I liked the look of her. Kate seemed rather unapproachable, but Rosie looked easygoing and uncritical. My suitcase was on my bed and I unpacked it quickly, hoping they wouldn't notice the blue leggings I was hanging at the darkest end of the closet weren't jodhpurs. Rosie was lounging on her bed, flicking through a magazine. Kate gathered up her pajamas and disappeared in the direction of the bathroom. Rosie smiled lazily at me.

"I'm tapped out after today's ride," she said ruefully, "and my butt hurts. I always forget riding's so painful to start with."

I clutched at a straw of hope. "You mean you don't go riding all the time?"

"If only!" sighed Rosie, dramatically. "No, we live in the middle of London. We only get to ride here."

"Do you come here a lot?"

"This is my second time, but Kate's been four times – she's older than me. I'm 13."

"Me too."

"Kate's nearly 15. She's one of the oldest here. There's Chris who's only 12 – he's the youngest – and a load of other boys who come from some school where they all like riding. Weird really, 'cause most boys hate riding once they get into high school, but it makes for a change, usually everyone here are girls. And there's Jane and Rachel – they've come together."

"What are they like?"

"OK, but they're best friends so they're wrapped up in each other. It'll be nice having you here so I don't have to be with Kate so much. She's OK, but she's my sister. And she's obsessed with boys."

"Are you a good rider?"

"That depends what you mean," answered Rosie, sitting cross-legged on the bed and groaning as her sore muscles objected. "If you call being able to canter without falling off good, then I am, but if you're thinking about pony club stuff, well... What's your riding like?'

I blushed. "I suppose I'm a bit like you, I live in a big town and riding lessons are too expensive." I took a deep breath. "I've never actually been on a horse."

Kate came back in at this point and let out a long whistle. "You'll have to work really hard," she said. "Everyone can ride quite well this week. You'll have to catch up fast."

I gulped. Rosie said kindly, "Don't worry – I was new to it last year, and I'm still here despite everything."

"Is there anything you'd like us to tell you about?" Kate sounded kind enough but I had the feeling she didn't really want to be bothered. And I was worried about so much, I didn't know where to begin. But there was one particular thing...

"What's it like when you fall off?"

Kate laughed. "You probably never will, and if you do, it doesn't have to hurt."

"It did last year when I came off that time," added Rosie. "Mr. Butler said I was winded – it feels awful, just like you're never going to be able to breathe again. You lie there, curled up in a heap, just gasping. It's horrible."

I stared at her in absolute terror. "Were you all right?"

"Course she was," said Kate casually. "Being winded's not serious, just a bit of a shock. It doesn't happen much. You'll be fine."

They didn't say much more. We got ready for bed and Kate turned out the light. I lay on my back and clutched the duvet cover tightly. I could see the faint outlines of the room and the shape of the window, but otherwise it was pretty dark and incredibly quiet, and I could hear from the others' even breathing that they were asleep. I felt sick. My stomach seemed full of wavering butterflies instead of pizza. My head was full of wild images of ponies crashing into six-foot walls and galloping uncontrollably over miles of open countryside, and I wished desperately that I could be transported magically back to my own safe bedroom, with the noise of traffic outside and the familiar whimpers from the twins in the next room. I drifted into sleep, and dreamt I was sitting on a giant horse, clutching a rein made mysteriously of grass, counting strides – one hundred and two, one hundred and three, one hundred and four, and knowing I was about to fall miles down to the hard stones below. It was almost a relief when I woke up, until I remembered where I was and what I was about to do.

Chapter 3

The corn flakes sat heavily in my stomach as I sidled into the yard. All around was happy confusion. Eleven assorted ponies were being saddled and bridled by eleven excited riders. Everyone knew exactly what to do.

As I watched, a picture flew into my mind of home. Home, as it might be this very moment, on a busy Tuesday morning. Dad would've left for work. I could see his empty cereal bowl as if it was real. Mom'd be cleaning up after the twins, washing up, maybe. Tim might be crawling round the floor with the squeaky toy car I'd given him at Christmas. He loves that car. And Holly might be trying to crawl after him, or she might still be smearing a soggy biscuit over her face, or she might be taking everything out of the saucepan cupboard and banging the lids together happily. Was anyone thinking about me? Were they imagining me having a wonderful time? Was Dad envying me being out in the country when he had to go to work as usual? Were Holly and Tim waiting for me to come through the door?

A tear slithered down my cheek. I felt lonelier and more miserable than I could ever remember, even worse than when the twins came home from hospital. I'd spent so much time and energy persuading Mom and Dad to let me come on this pony vacation. If only I could go back into the past and change their decision, and not have to be here at all.

Mr. Butler's voice startled me. "Come on, then, Jessica, where've you been? Your pony's still in the paddock." He looked at me closely and smiled. "Feeling a bit new? Never mind, you'll be fine. Tell you what, shall I catch him for you and then I'll show you how to tack up."

I nodded. I didn't trust my voice not to tremble. I stayed in my corner while Mr. Butler vaulted over a gate into the paddock beyond. A moment later he was back, unlatching the gate this time, leading a pony.

My pony! I'd been so bound up with worries and homesickness that I'd actually forgotten about the ponies. And this was to be mine for a whole week! He was almost white (gray, I told myself sternly; all white ponies are called gray) and not too big, with a delicate way of walking and the prettiest face. His mane and tail were long and flowing and his eyes brown and gentle. I was enchanted. I forgot everything else and ran over to hug him.

The pony was startled by my sudden rush and skittered nervously. Mr. Butler kept a strong hand on the rope bridle and soothed him, while I watched, feeling a bit foolish.

"Gently, now," he said. "Your pony's called Tim, and he'll soon get to know you, but you mustn't tear up to him like that."

Tim! I felt warmed by the coincidence and put out a hand towards his nose. He harrumphed softly and pushed his warm nostrils against my hand.

"He's greedy," said Mr. Butler. "All that grass overnight, and he's still looking for tidbits. Right, go and get his saddle and bridle from the tack room and I'll show you what to do."

I followed his pointing finger to a shed where a saddle and bridle hung on a peg marked "Tim." All the other pegs were empty. As I came out, I could see that almost everyone else was ready, so I hurried over to Tim, but I slowed down as I came close so as not to scare him again.

"That's right," said Mr. Butler. "Now, what do you know about these?"

25

I swallowed nervously. "Not much," I said in a voice that came out small, "just what I've read in books."

"Not had much to do with ponies then?" he asked, as he lifted the saddle easily over Tim's back and reached under him to get the girth, the strap that tightens the saddle.

"Not much," I said again. I wasn't going to admit I'd never actually touched a pony till this morning. I watched Mr. Butler tighten the buckle and slip two fingers between the girth and Tim's skin.

"Not too tight," he explained, "otherwise he'll get sore. But not too loose or you'll fall off!"

I giggled nervously. Now Mr. Butler was slipping the complicated web of leather and metal over Tim's head. In an instant, it seemed, all was in place, even a steel bar that had somehow got into Tim's mouth. I couldn't for the life of me see how he'd done it.

"One thing at a time," Mr. Butler said, with a friendly smile. "I'll expect you to do the saddle yourself next time, and I'll show you the bridle again tomorrow. Whatever you do, don't take off the rope head collar or you'll never catch him again. Oh, and you haven't met Caroline, have you? She's my assistant. Ask her if you need any help."

He waved a hand towards a girl of about 18 who seemed to bulge out of every part of her clothes; even her riding hat balanced on top of very fair hair that sprang out at the sides like a clown's. She was checking the line of waiting ponies and riders.

"OK, everyone, lunch packs in the saddle bags over there, buckle them on, hats on properly, and mount."

Oh no! Another thing I'd done wrong. Dad had arranged for me to borrow a hard riding hat, but no one had said anything about it and I'd completely forgotten. I blushed bright red and touched Mr. Butler's arm.

"I ... er ... haven't got a hat yet. Dad said..."

27

"Oh, yes, we're lending you one." Mr. Butler made my fears seem silly again. "Run along to the tack room again. There are some hats in a box. Make sure it fits."

All around me, ponies were being mounted expertly, reins gathered into capable hands, feet thrust confidently into stirrups. I threaded through the confusion back to the shed, and found the box with its jumble of hats. It took a few tries to find one that fitted and my fingers shook as I did up the chinstrap. It felt odd, much harder and stiffer than I'd expected, but I looked at my reflection in a window and I looked really cool, just like a proper rider. I noticed some leather riding crops and took one. Real riders use them all the time. I went back to the yard. Everyone else was on their ponies now and they were all watching me. My mind raced. Which side should I stand to get on to Tim? I knew, I just knew, it was one particular side but which? Then, as I got close, Caroline, who was holding his reins, quietly indicated that I should go to Tim's left side, and equally quietly murmured instructions to me as she steadied his head.

"That's it now, face the back and put your left foot in the stirrup. Go on, now, reach up, you can do it, he's not very tall. There. Now, put your hands on the saddle – hold the reins in your left hand – ready? Now, spring!"

To my utter amazement, I found myself, for the first time in my life, sitting on a pony. A warm, sweet scent came from him. His mane was much rougher than I'd expected, but his gray coat looked soft and smooth; I didn't dare let go of the saddle actually to stroke it. He stood patiently while Caroline adjusted the stirrups on their straps – they're called leathers – to the right length.

"Remember, fourth hole from the top," she said. She tightened Tim's girth again and showed me how to hold the reins. I had to have them just right, not so loose that they flapped but not so tight that Tim could only move his head a little bit.

The only hard thing really was getting my fingers right. The reins had to sort of thread through my fingers, with the little fingers different from the rest, and that felt odd. Once I was organized, Caroline smiled encouragingly.

"You'll be fine," she said. I'd dropped the riding crop on the ground, but when Caroline noticed it she said I wasn't allowed a stick until I was more experienced. She took it back to the tack room and fetched a saddlebag for me, as I'd forgotten, and attached it to the side of the saddle.

Mr. Butler was waiting impatiently by his own horse, which was tall and chestnut brown and impressive looking, tacked up ready by the yard entrance. "OK, all of you, follow me – and single file till we're off the lanes. Remember, keep a pony's length away from each other and Mike, watch out that Bilbo doesn't nip."

He swung himself onto his horse's back with enviable ease, and without any obvious move on his part, it set off. All around me, the other ponies followed. My mind went blank. What on earth do you do to get a pony going? I thought. Then I saw Rosie kicking her heels energetically into her pony's sides, just behind the girth, and I remembered the pony books. Of course, you squeeze the pony's sides and it'll go. I squeezed tentatively and nothing happened. Then I tried again – still nothing. They'd all left the yard now. Tears rose up in my eyes but I didn't dare let go of the reins to wipe them away. I whispered "Sorry Tim, I don't want to hurt you," and bounced my heels against his sides as hard as I dared.

Quietly and calmly, Tim walked after the other ponies. My hands dropped automatically to grab the front of the saddle but I managed to keep hold of the reins as well. The motion of the pony was quite different from what I'd expected; he sort of swayed one side forward and then the other. But I wasn't falling off, and I was catching the others up as they

29

plodded down the lane, and at last I was actually, really, riding!

It was a few minutes before I felt secure enough to relax my tight grip on the saddle and look around. We were spread out in a long line along the narrow lane, all close to the hedge, with Mr. Butler at the front, and Rosie on a lovely sturdy chestnut (that's glossy brown) pony just ahead of me. There was a soothing rhythm to the ponies' gentle walk. I felt incredibly pleased with myself.

The procession slowed down. I knew from my books that I should pull on the reins to slow Tim, so I did. To my frustration, though, he stopped dead and dropped his head alarmingly to the ground to tear a mouthful of grass from the verge. I only just saved myself from going straight over his head and the reins shot painfully through my fingers. I sat back up and kicked helplessly at Tim's sides, tugging at the reins, while he munched on. All the other ponies were still walking on and were turning through a gateway into a grassy field. I held on to the saddle as tightly as I could and tried kicking again. Tim took one step forward, barely lifting his head from the ground, and then stopped. I could feel my face burning with embarrassment as I tried again. This time he ignored me completely.

There was a clatter of hooves from behind. Caroline trotted up on a brown and white pony that was almost as fat as her.

"Stuck?" she said sympathetically. "Let's see – first, pull his head up, and then loosen the reins just a little bit or he'll think he's got to stand still. Let them run through your fingers – that's right. Now, kick on."

As she spoke, she leaned over and gave Tim a hefty smack with her riding crop. To my delight, Tim moved smoothly forward and Caroline came alongside, giving advice as she went.

"Sit up really straight so your heels go down," she said. "You can hold on to the saddle till you get your balance but don't let go of the reins. Now – hey, where are you going?" Tim had carried straight on past the gateway.

I struggled to pull the reins to stop him. Caroline told me to pull on the right rein and kick. Tim turned, so sharply that I lost my balance and grabbed the saddle with one hand and his mane with the other. The reins hung loose as Tim wandered into the field, and I was nearly caught out again as his head shot down to the grass taking his mane – and my fingers – with it. I just stopped myself from sliding down his neck headfirst to the ground. My cheeks itching-red, I glanced around. Yes, just as I'd expected. Everyone was looking and there was loads of giggling. Never in my whole life had I felt such a fool. Mr. Butler was grinning widely, too. How dare they? I thought, anger welling up inside me. Is it my fault I'm a beginner?

But Mr. Butler was nice, and showed me again how to pick up the reins and tug Tim's head up, and much to my surprise Tim obeyed. The rest of the group, led by Caroline, set off across the fields, towards some woods. The first few broke into a trot, but Mr. Butler leaned down and grabbed Tim's bridle before he could join in. "Not just yet," he said. "Don't worry, I'll hold him."

My anger subsided as I began to feel more in control. Things felt different on the grass after the tarmac lane – it was quieter, of course, and the movement was mostly smoother, though once or twice Tim stumbled and I had to grab a handful of mane very fast. Mr. Butler left me to it, and soon I was trailing along at the rear again, glad no one was watching. I tried to copy what the others were doing, though it was hard from behind, and soon we'd crossed the field.

We went along a narrow, rutted track. Tim was quite happily following the other ponies now, so I concentrated on sit-

31

ting securely and holding the reins as well as the saddle. It's surprising how wide a pony's back is; it's not a bit like sitting on a bike. But although it's so wide, it wobbles an awful lot, and there are all sorts of bumps and wriggles which feel really dangerous at first, until after a bit you realize they don't really matter. I was just feeling really happy for the first time when Tim stopped dead. I lurched forward, grabbing bits of mane yet again, and then sat back and kicked. Nothing happened. I kicked Tim's sides gently – I was afraid he'd be hating me – and I could feel hot tears getting ready to spill from my eyes and embarrass me even more. Then Caroline looked around and yelled, "Stand up in the stirrups while he stales!"

I didn't have the faintest idea what she was talking about. How do you stand up on a horse, and anyway what's staling? Then I heard a loud trickling noise and saw a big smelly puddle, and I realized that Tim was peeing – and you wouldn't believe how much pee a pony can produce. Caroline trotted over and showed me what to do – you stand up so your feet are in the stirrups but your bottom's not putting any pressure on the pony's back, and you have to accept that for a few minutes the pony can't walk anywhere. In fact, when I saw other ponies doing it, it was quite funny as the pony sort of sticks its back legs out sideways and concentrates really hard, and quite often the riders don't realize at first and bounce up and down kicking like mad and getting nowhere – it wasn't just me that looked a fool sometimes.

As we turned a corner into thick woods, the track led down quite steeply. Mr. Butler had reined in and was waiting for me.

"Lean back a bit," he advised, "so your pony doesn't lose his balance, and concentrate on holding on with your legs."

Tim lurched down the track at a really scary fast walk, though leaning back helped. My legs wanted to stick out in front, so I had to work hard to glue them to Tim's sides. That did help my balance, though. It felt a bit like swaying in a back to front hammock. The track widened out at the bottom of the hill and the riders started to group themselves in twos and threes. I was surprised to find Kate next to me, riding a piebald pony with casual grace.

"How you doing?"

I blushed. "Not that well. I keep getting left behind. Tim never wants to go where I want."

"You're not giving him the right signals," explained Kate. "You'll get the hang of it soon."

"It's easy for you. You've been riding for ages," I said enviously.

"Me? All I've had is four weeks here over two years. That's not much. Rosie and me came together last autumn half term, and we got Mom and Dad to let us come again this year, but we had to earn most of it – loads of car washing and baby-sitting."

"Even Rosie can ride much better than me," I commented gloomily.

Kate laughed. "Give yourself a chance. She's a good week ahead of you. By the end of this week you'll be cantering."

"It's trotting that's bothering me. All that stuff about rising trot. I've read about it, and I thought it'd be easy. But nothing's quite like you imagine."

"Why not try letting go of the saddle now we're on the flat?" Kate suggested. "If you sit up straight and keep your heels down, you won't wobble."

I gritted my teeth and let go. Nothing terrible happened. I felt insecure at first, but a moment later I'd tuned in to the pony's rhythm and it felt easy and natural. I smiled at Kate happily.

"What next?"

"Try to steer more," advised Kate. "You just pull on the

33

rein the side you want to go and squeeze that side's leg as well."

I tried but nothing happened. Kate laughed.

"You mustn't hurt him, but you don't have to be that gentle – he can't feel a thing. OK, try to go off the track here to the right and back again round that tree."

It's not that easy, I thought, but I tugged the right rein and squeezed with my right leg, and, to my amazement, Tim calmly left the procession and went where I intended. As we passed the tree, I pulled the left rein and pushed with my left knee, and we were back on the track.

Kate looked really pleased.

"Thanks a million," I said. "I can't believe this, I'm really riding. I've dreamed of this forever."

"Just like us," said Kate. "We both wanted to ride at home, but we live in the middle of London and it costs much too much."

I began to tell Kate the story of how I'd managed to come on the trek. I hardly noticed that we'd come out of the woods onto open moorland. The track wound upwards steeply and was very rough. Sitting quite relaxed as Tim picked his way through the ruts, I was telling Kate about the day the magic numbers came up when Tim stumbled heavily. My feet jerked from the stirrups, I let go of the reins as his head shot forward, and I rolled over his shoulder into an uncomfortable heap on the ground.

Kate halted her pony and slid off quickly. "You OK?" she asked, pulling me up. "You went down with quite a bump."

Mr. Butler came trotting back. He jumped down and caught Tim, who was, predictably, happily grazing a few paces away.

"It was Tim's fault," I told him. "I was doing everything right, like you and Kate told me, and he suddenly jumped forward and made me fall off."

"Are you hurt?"

"No," I said, half-wishing I was.

"She came off quite slowly," put in Kate. "We were talking, and not paying attention, so when Tim tripped..."

"I'm glad to see that you've learned one of the golden rules of horsemanship, Kate," said Mr. Butler. "That, Jessica, is that it's never – or hardly ever – the pony's fault when something goes wrong."

"But it's not my fault if he doesn't watch where he's going, is it?"

"Ah, that's what riding's all about. You're supposed to notice what he's doing and where he's going."

"Everyone else was talking," I said. "Their ponies didn't make them fall and, I've been trying *so* hard this morning."

Mr. Butler smiled. "Tim didn't 'make' you fall," he said. "You didn't watch where you were going, so you didn't guide him around the rough parts, and you weren't ready when he stumbled. Anyway, you're all right, and you're not the first person to fall off, or make a silly mistake, for that matter. Get up on him again now."

Without thinking I went to Tim's right side to remount.

"Wrong side," said Mr. Butler, not unkindly, but I felt very silly as I went all the way around to Tim's other side. Because of the slope, the stirrup was now a very long way for my foot to reach. I hung onto the saddle and stretched my leg up and just managed to get my toes in. Then I tried to jump up into the saddle, but Tim chose that moment to take a step forward. I had to hop along trying to keep up with him. To make things worse, I heard a muffled giggle from Kate behind me.

"Have another try," said Mr. Butler, already back on his horse, leaning over and grabbing Tim's bridle to steady him. I gritted my teeth and jumped again. The muscles in my left leg felt stretched to bursting, but I heaved myself up till my body lay over the saddle, and swung my right foot over Tim's back and down into the stirrup again.

"Now get yourself properly organized before you start," said Mr. Butler. "Fingers through the reins, feet well down in the stirrups, nice straight back – that's it! Kick on, now."

I'll show that I can do it on my own, even if I did fall off, I thought. I settled myself in the saddle and gave Tim a good, firm kick. To my horror, he took off. At a fast trot, he chased after the other riders, who were well ahead by this time, with me clinging on to mane, saddle and reins. My bottom was bouncing rapidly on the hard leather saddle, and I skidded from side to side as I landed from each lurching bounce. My hat came forward over my eyes but I didn't have a hand free to push it back. Then my right foot slipped out of its stirrup, and I just knew I'd fall off. But luckily Tim decided to slow down as he neared the other ponies. He subsided into a walk. Panting and sweaty, I maneuvered my foot back in the stirrup and pushed my riding hat back.

Kate and Mr. Butler trotted up from behind, neat and organized. Kate was in fits of giggles, which I thought very unkind, and Mr. Butler also seemed to be trying to hide a smile.

"Your first trot!" was all he said, as he trotted past to the front of the moving column.

Kate was still spurting with laughter. I ignored her. Then I saw Rosie ahead, one hand on the reins, the other planted on her pony's back so that she could turn round and watch.

"Hey, Jess," Rosie called, "you looked like a sack of potatoes, all bouncing and falling about!"

"Thanks *very* much," I muttered. We were walking sedately now, gently downwards. A couple of the other riders were also turning to look at me. I sat stiffly upright. I was determined not to make a fool of myself any more.

"You'll be cantering this afternoon!" called Rosie, turning away as she spoke.

Cantering? If I could've got off and run home that second, I would have. I still felt sick from all that jolting, and a bit scared, but cantering! That was really fast. I'd never be able to do that.

I barely noticed that all the ponies, including Tim, were stopping. I just managed to steady myself in time as Tim's head went down to the grass.

"OK, everyone, lunch!" called Mr. Butler. "Tether your ponies over there." He indicated a length of fence, which bordered a fast-running stream with steep rocky banks. "Make sure they get a drink first."

Everyone else slid off their ponies and led them along to a place where the stream widened and the bank was gentler. How was I supposed to get down? The only way I knew was to fall off.

"Well, you've already dismounted once, but this time we'll do it properly." Mr. Butler appeared by my side. "Both feet out of the stirrups, swing the right foot over the back of the saddle – *don't* kick the poor pony's back – and drop to the ground. Easy, eh?"

It was. He showed me how to run the stirrups up the leathers so they wouldn't annoy Tim, and how to loosen the girth a bit. He took off Tim's bridle so that he could graze without a bit in his mouth, and told me to lead him to the fence, careful to keep my feet clear in case he trod on me. I let my pony drink, and tied the long rope that was still attached to his head collar to the fence and left him to graze. As I walked away, I couldn't help thinking it would be nice never to see Tim again. My legs and bottom were sore, my shoulder was bruised from the fall, and I was sure everyone would spend the entire lunch break laughing at me and teasing me. And then, this afternoon, cantering.

Chapter 4

Everyone was lounging on the short grass. I sidled over to a fallen tree trunk and opened my lunch, carefully avoiding everyone else's eyes. But I listened to the conversation, and was quite surprised to hear it was about all sorts of things – football, music, school, families – and not at all about silly beginners who couldn't control their ponies. Feeling bolder, I ate a sandwich. The fresh, clean air had made me hungry and I quickly ate another, then another.

"How's it going?" Rosie flopped down next to me.

"Oh, you know," I muttered. "I did most things wrong."

"Not when I was watching," said Rosie, surprisingly. "Mostly you did fine. It was only when Tim trotted, you weren't ready and you didn't know how to rise. I'll show you later, or Mr. Butler will."

"Or Caroline. She's been really nice."

My spirits rose. I remembered the good parts of the morning, when I'd been in control.

Kate came over with a boy. "This is Ed," she said, "Sorry I laughed at you, but it was funny when you shot off like that. You should've seen your face!"

I started to feel bad again, but Ed said, "You did OK. I haven't forgotten what it's like to be a beginner even if *she* has. And I fell off twice yesterday." He smiled encouragingly and I felt comforted. He had warm brown eyes under spiky hair and was really good-looking.

"I bet you're sore today, then," Kate giggled.

"No worse than you'll be in a minute!"

Ed grabbed Kate and started to tickle her ribs. She squirmed away giggling and for a charged moment they stared at each other.

"I'll get you!" she yelled, and chased him along the rough grass. He cleared the stream at a narrow point in one leap and pranced around laughing on the other side, daring Kate to follow. She hesitated. The stream was quite deep, with awkwardly shaped sharp rocks breaking the flow into bubbly trails. The grass banks were smooth and slippery, sloping steeply into the water.

"Chicken!" taunted Ed from the opposite bank. Everyone was watching Kate; even the ponies had lifted their heads from the turf to see what was happening.

"Go for it, Kate!" shouted Rosie, next to me, and I heard myself shouting, "Go on!"

Kate took a couple of steps backwards, then one pace forward and jumped. For a split second, it looked as if she was going to make it; but at the last moment, her outstretched foot couldn't quite reach the opposite bank, and with a resounding splash she was spread-eagled in the water.

"It's freezing!" she yelped. "Help me, Ed!"

Still laughing, Ed reached down his hand. Kate took it, but she pulled him off balance and he landed in the stream with a terrific smack.

"Get out of the water, both of you!" shouted Caroline feebly. She clambered down the bank, but they were far too busy floundering around and splashing each other and laughing to take any notice.

"Where did Mr. Butler go?" asked the boy next to me. He looked really worried. "This is getting beyond a joke."

Rosie was hopping about at the top of the slope, shouting encouragement to her sister. The tall boy who'd teased the young one at supper the night before started a rhythmic chant – "E –ed, E – ed. E – ed!"

"Break it up! Mr. Butler's coming!" called the boy next to me. He hadn't joined in the chanting. I looked around and saw Mr. Butler striding across the field, wiping his mouth with his hand. Within moments, the crowd had melted away. Too engrossed to notice, Kate and Ed were smacking great handfuls of water at each other. Mr. Butler pushed past everyone, leapt down the bank, waded straight out into the water, grabbed them, one in each hand, and yanked them apart. They were soaked to the skin.

"Get out!" ordered Mr. Butler, and they splashed to the edge and stood dripping, giggling weakly, on the grass. "What a pair of idiots!" he said, looking from one to the other. "I must be a headcase, bringing a lot of hooligans like you out into the wilds. Can't you be trusted for just five minutes while I have a drink?"

"Sorry, sir," Kate and Ed spoke together.

"OK, we'll have to get you two sorted out," he said. "Can't have you spending the rest of the day in wet clothes, not in April." He turned to Caroline. "Take charge while I get these two back to the farm, OK?"

"Do you want me to start the ride?"

"No, no," said Mr. Butler. "I'll only be an hour – if we hack straight back along the lanes it's not far from the farm. This morning's route was a big circle. I'll take your Micky, Caroline; it's not good for Captain to trot along the roads. You go and phone home from the pub to say I'm coming, will you? It won't hurt the ponies to have a longer rest." He looked at the rest of us fiercely. "Just all stay here, and no one's to go near that stream."

He untied three ponies, and hustled Kate and Ed away.

40

Kate was shivering in the cool wind, and Ed was rubbing his back where the sharp rocks had bruised him, but they looked surprisingly cheerful.

Rosie nudged me. "Well, Kate got what she wanted."

"What do you mean?"

"She's had a crush on Ed ever since we got here. You wait – they'll spend all their time together from now on."

"What a bunch of idiots," said the boy by me in disgust. "They could've gotten hurt."

"Don't be such a spoilsport," said Rosie. "Don't you ever have fights with your brothers?"

"I'm an only child," he replied, rather smugly.

"That explains it, then," said Rosie cheerfully. "It's only people who don't have any brothers or sisters that get all heated over a silly fight like that. Kate and me are always bickering, when we're not best friends, that is."

She wandered off, leaving me with the boy. He smiled. "I'm Phil," he said. He looked nice – quite tall with curly brown hair and freckles and a gentle expression. I felt flattered that he wanted to be friends. We sat down and I took off my sweater, folded it into a pillow, and laid back. The sun was flitting in and out of clouds, but it was surprisingly warm for April.

"Do *you* have lots of brothers and sisters?" Phil asked suddenly.

"No, I'm an only ... except..." For a moment, I'd completely forgotten the twins' existence.

"What do you mean?" Phil asked – but just then we heard some noise which caught our attention. I sat up. Mike, looking dangerous, was standing over the younger boy of the night before. A semi-circle of other boys stood behind Mike, egging him on. Chris, sitting alone with his sandwiches, was looking defiant.

Phil whistled quietly. "Here goes," he said. "More trouble."

41

We stood up and joined the rest. Everyone was quiet, watching and listening.

"Well, now," said Mike, a note of menace in his voice. "Here's your chance. Mr. Butler should be gone a good hour and that fat slob Caroline's gone off to use the phone. What better chance could there be to prove you're right – or wrong?"

"What if I won't?"

"Oh, I think you will," said Mike. "We'd be so disappointed if you chickened out – wouldn't we?" The boys around Mike nodded eagerly. "Otherwise we could make life really unpleasant for you for the rest of the week, couldn't we?"

I whispered urgently to Phil, "Isn't there anything we can do?"

"Not now," he hissed back. "It's mostly his own fault anyway, he was showing off like mad yesterday and it got to Mike."

Chris seemed to be considering. Suddenly, he jumped to his feet, scattering sandwich crumbs, and stepped right up to Mike, who looked twice as tall as him.

"OK," he said. "I said I could ride anything here. Which one d'you want me on?"

Mike swiveled on his heel and surveyed the line of tied-up ponies. The biggest was Bilbo, the thin black pony that he'd been riding, and he slapped his rump and seemed about to pick him. But then he went on to the end of the line, where Mr. Butler's tall chestnut horse was fidgeting.

"Captain," he said simply.

Chris gulped. He's going to refuse, I thought, and couldn't decide if I'd be relieved or sorry if he did.

"OK," he said, and went over.

Mike's gang clustered round him. Rosie, Phil, me and the two other girls – Rachel and Jane – drifted uneasily together.

Rosie said in a jittery voice, "I'm sure it's dangerous for

42

him to try to ride Captain. He's really powerful, and he's used to a heavy rider who can control him."

"I don't see how he'll even get up, he's so small," murmured Rachel, as Chris untied Captain and pulled down the stirrup. He had to stretch to his fullest just to reach the buckle to make the stirrup leather longer. He undid it and pulled the stirrup down, but then he couldn't do the buckle up again. He looked around despairingly. Mike was behind him, but he wasn't going to offer any help.

I suddenly remembered how my brother Tim had been when he first learned to sit up. He fell over dozens of times, but each time he doggedly pulled himself back up to a sitting position until he finally got the knack. Almost forgetting that it was now Chris and not Tim that was struggling bravely, I pushed Mike to one side, and reached up. I could just reach the buckle to do it up securely.

I looked down at Chris. I'm not that tall myself, but he really was small. "D'you want a leg-up?" I heard myself saying.

Mike grabbed my T-shirt and pulled me backwards. "Keep out of it, new girl," he growled.

I looked at him. His eyes were narrow, and his face pale with anger. I was far more scared than in the morning, when all I'd dreaded was the riding. Then a contrasting picture of my baby brother Tim with his big, trusting blue eyes came into my head. "Don't be stupid," I said. Chris balanced for a split second on my joined hands, pushed off, got a foot into the stirrup, then hauled himself into the saddle, though his feet barely reached the top of the saddle flaps.

"Thanks," he said, flashing a smile as he shortened the leathers as far as they'd go.

"That's cool." I flicked around, ignoring Mike's heavy, menacing breathing, and went back to Rosie and the others, a glow of pride bubbling inside me.

"That wasn't exactly smart," said Rosie. "He'll have it in for you now, too." She gulped as if she was trying not to cry. "I wish we'd never come. It's never been like this before."

"Sssh," said Phil. Chris was sitting very upright in the saddle, gathering the reins in his fingers. Captain wore a double bridle, which meant there were two lines of leather to manage with his small hands, but you could see his determination winning through.

"So, where d'you want me to go?" he asked Mike, completely nonchalant.

"Forget it," said Mike scathingly. "The bet's off. Babyface here didn't mount on his own, did he?"

There was a ripple of laughter. I felt tense with frustration and anger, but Chris grinned. "The bet was to ride him, that's all," he said. "So I'll ride him. Where?"

Mike shrugged his shoulders. "Up to you," he said. "Doesn't bother me."

He turned and walked along the riverbank, away from the ponies, his friends hurrying after him.

Chris kicked hard and flapped the reins to get Captain moving. He caught up with Mike and said, "Look, I'm riding. I've kept my side of the bargain."

One of Mike's friends nudged him and said something.

"OK," Mike said grudgingly, "the bet's still on. But you have to prove you really can ride him."

"No problem."

Mike glanced round at the wild landscape, considering. "I want you cantering him, jumping the stream, going up that hill, and galloping him back down over the stone wall and the stream. Fast."

I clutched Rosie's arm. "Can he do it?"

"Maybe," Rosie whispered. "But it's not a very safe course to try even on a pony you know and the right size for you. Would you fancy jumping that stream?"

45

I shook my head. We watched, fascinated, as Chris got Captain first to walk, then to trot, and then to canter along the smooth grass.

"Chris is a pain," Jane said, "but he's got guts. It'll be a long way to fall."

Chris hauled on the reins and turned Captain towards the water. The horse obviously didn't like the look of it and danced sideways, kicking his heels. Chris bounced and jerked but clung on. He lifted both legs and clapped them in against Captain's sides, and at the same time struck Captain's neck with the reins. A muted cheer came from my group as Captain lifted effortlessly over the stream, clearing the vicious rocks, and landed sweetly on the other side. Mike glared at us.

Captain shot up the hill on the opposite side. It was steep and slippery, with scraggy bushes and patches of bare stone. Once Captain's back feet skidded dramatically, and Rachel screamed as he lurched sideways with a scrabbling of hooves on rock that sent sparks flying. Chris clung on somehow. His light weight was a positive advantage uphill, but when they reached the top and wheeled around to face the treacherous downward slope, even I could see that it would be hard for Chris to control the heavy horse in any way.

"Just so long as he sticks on..." breathed Rosie.

"And doesn't ruin the horse's legs," added Phil gloomily. "Can you imagine what Mr. Butler's going to say when he finds out what's been going on?"

"As if anyone would tell him!" retorted Rosie.

Chris was poised, ready to go. Coming down at a walk would be tricky enough, but galloping was the height of stupidity, and we all knew it. We watched breathlessly as Chris slapped the horse with his heels, shook the reins, and leaned forward.

There was no sound except for the steady pounding of

hooves that turned into thunder as Captain tore down the slope, twisting sideways now and then to avoid any obstacles, with Chris almost completely still on his back, just his hands moving as he guided the horse as best he could. I found myself clenching my fists so hard that my fingernails hurt the skin of my hands. Our eyes were glued to the boy perched on the enormous, powerful animal. Rosie was holding me, with a grip that was bruising my arm, but I hardly noticed as the canter became a headlong gallop, straight towards the leg-breaking stone wall that lay straight in their path. Surely Captain would fall, or at the very least, Chris would be thrown, and would lie, limp as a rag doll, at the edge of the stream.

Chapter 5

Two things happened almost at once. A yell of "Stop, you idiot!" jerked everyone's head round to see Caroline running full pelt towards us waving her arms frantically. Then, like puppets pulled by strings, we all twisted back to watch Chris. The wall loomed ahead of Captain and then he'd have to clear the stream, narrower but deep and studded with rocks. Breathing became impossible. The world stopped in its tracks. There was nothing that mattered except for Chris and Captain, and I just knew that disaster was a moment away.

The silence was broken by a wordless yell from Chris as he leaned forward over Captain's neck and kicked his sides with all his strength. They were so close now that it seemed impossible Captain could jump in time, and he'd never be able to stop. I shut my eyes – I just couldn't watch – all I could hear was the pounding hooves and then silence. Against my will, my eyes opened, and there, filling the whole sky, was the massive horse and his tiny rider soaring up and over the stone wall and the stream in one beautiful, graceful arc. It was total magic.

Caroline grabbed the sweating horse's reins as he stamped and danced excitedly.

"Get down this instant!" she ordered, her voice shaky with anger. "What on earth gave you the idea you could ride Captain? Thank God, it doesn't look as if you've damaged

him. And you could have been killed – it would serve you right if you had been. What's going on here? First that fight and now this..." She turned on us and pointed at Rosie. "OK, you, tell me, what's going on?"

Rosie hesitated. "Chris wanted to see if he could manage a big horse," she said awkwardly. "So he thought he'd have a try..."

"And what about the rest of you? Didn't anyone have the sense to stop him? Who's the oldest? Mike…?"

Mike sauntered over. "Sorry, Caroline," he said. "I never knew what he was doing till he'd started."

"But..." I started, but Jane pulled at me.

"Don't make it worse," she whispered. "Caroline's calming down – look."

It was true. She'd examined Captain's legs and found no injury, and Chris had slipped down and was standing by Captain, patting his neck. He was looking very pleased with himself.

"I half-wish he'd fallen off and broken his neck," sighed Rosie. "He'll be so cocky now. He was enough of a show-off before."

"Especially if Mike lets him join his gang," added Phil gloomily.

It wasn't long before Mr. Butler cantered back on Caroline's sturdy pony. He called to everyone to pack away lunch and remount. He seemed quite short-tempered already, but it didn't look as if Caroline was going to make things worse by telling him what had happened while he was away. I thought she probably didn't want to look as if she couldn't control us.

I didn't want to ask either of them for help getting Tim ready but Phil helped me put the bridle back on, tighten the girth, and mount. Phil's own pony was a lively bay (that means she had a light brown body but dark brown mane and

50

tail) called Bramble, and he had to jump about to get up on her as she was sidestepping and annoying other ponies.

"Control that pony!" came Mr. Butler's voice, and Phil blushed and grabbed the reins. I hung on tightly to Tim's reins and a handful of mane and watched the others carefully. Mr. Butler was now back on Captain and trotted along the line of ponies checking that everyone was ready. As he passed me he nodded and said, "It'll be a short ride this afternoon after all this delay. You'll manage fine. I'll give you a hand with rising trot soon. And let go of the poor pony's mane. How would you like to be held on to by your hair? Balance properly, or if you can't, hold on to the pommel on the front of the saddle. OK?"

"OK," I muttered. We were all rather subdued, except for Chris who was sitting bolt upright on his little New Forest gray, a broad grin of triumph all over his face. Mike, at the rear, looked irritable and fidgety.

We set off along the stream that had caused so much drama, and clattered across it at a shallow bit. At the middle, Tim put his head down to drink, but I was concentrating hard. I jerked the reins and kicked and, with a flurry of hooves, he broke into a trot and splashed out of the water. I hung on tightly to the pommel and felt pleased with myself. I'm learning to be a proper rider, I thought.

Meanwhile, Bramble was still playing up and was dancing sideways at the far side of the stream, pretending she didn't dare to cross. Phil was looking hot and bothered, whacking Bramble's sides with his heels and slapping her neck with his hand. Mr. Butler, who'd been at the head of the column, cantered back and re-crossed the stream. "Giddy up!" he shouted, and gave Bramble a hefty slap on her back. Startled, she shot across the stream like a rocket, Phil clinging on around her neck with his feet out of their stirrups. Everyone laughed at him, but it was a more cheerful and re-

51

laxed group after that, except for Phil who looked cross and sulky at being the butt of the joke.

For ages, we followed a winding path up and down grassy hills. We went at a walk, in single file. No one talked much, though every now and then Rosie would turn in the saddle and give me a word of encouragement. Phil was still having some trouble with his pony, but Tim plodded along in line quite happily, so I could concentrate on holding the reins correctly and sitting properly. The only horrible thing that happened was when Twinkle suddenly lifted his tail and let a whole pile of disgusting poop drop onto the track right in front of us, so close that it nearly splashed onto Tim's nose. And they all seemed to think that was perfectly OK, and that it was my fault for letting Tim get too close.

Eventually the path wound downwards and we entered a long, narrow valley, with a wide line of grass down the middle and trees on either side. Mr. Butler halted us and told everyone to get off for a moment.

"We'll just give the ponies a minute's rest and check girths before going along here," he said. "It's time to do some faster work. The good riders get a canter in here."

There was a murmur of excitement. I patted Tim's soft nose and rubbed my cheek against his lovely sweet-smelling neck. The girth was firm and I knew how to mount, but the butterflies were flying back at the thought of "fast work."

We scrambled back onto our ponies, some more elegantly than others, at Mr. Butler's command. "Right," he said, " I know we've got at least one person here who's not ready to canter. Who else isn't very confident?"

To my surprise, three others put up their hands – Jane, and two of Mike's friends – though they looked a bit embarrassed.

"Over here, the four of you, then," said Mr. Butler. "Now, the rest of you can trot on when I say, but keep in single file

52

so the ponies don't think they're racing. Then when you get to that oak tree, kick on to a canter to the end of the valley. Phil, you keep Bramble at the back and make sure you're in control; she's in a very nervous mood today." He looked around the group and pointed. "You, Rachel, isn't it? You lead. You seem to be more in control than some people. Caroline, keep at the rear and help any stragglers."

He still sounded cross, which made me nervous. Would he be very difficult if I didn't get trotting right?

He told the better riders to set off and turned to me.

"It's not hard to trot, once you've got the rhythm going," he said, "but some people take a while to get that. It should feel quite natural and light if you're rising properly, so if it does-n't, you've probably got it wrong. Right, walk on in line."

We kicked our ponies obediently and walked after the oth-ers, who were now trotting along neatly, bottoms rising and falling in unison with their ponies. Suddenly they all broke into a fast canter and whizzed away down the valley. It was so cool. I watched open-mouthed; there was nothing I want-ed more at that moment than to be able to fly along like that.

"Control your ponies!" instructed Mr. Butler. "They'll want to follow the others."

We all held the reins in tightly. Tim did a little enthusias-tic jump, which made me wobble, but I hung on with my knees clamped to the saddle.

"Now you can all trot on to join the others. Jessica, hold on to the saddle if you like. Now kick on and try to go with the pony."

I half-kicked but Tim started anyway because the pony in front did. He was eager to go faster, but I felt distinctly un-comfortable. I seemed to be bouncing incredibly fast, and couldn't feel any of this natural, easy movement Mr. Butler had described. He'd been helping Adam behind me but now he came up by me and watched for a second or two.

"Try to rise when I say," he suggested, and then went, "Rise ... rise ... rise ... rise" at surprisingly long intervals. I struggled to obey. At first I crashed back into the saddle at the most painful moment, but then I caught the sweet rhythm, and though I lost it again almost at once, I saw what I was aiming at and tried again and managed to go most of the rest of the way to the other ponies, at a smooth, neat rising trot. It was incredible.

We were all crowded together, talking excitedly, and I didn't notice that Mike had maneuvered Bilbo around behind me. The next thing I knew Tim had suddenly skittered wildly, scattering the other ponies. Voices were raised in protest but I wasn't there to hear them. Tim had decided he wanted to leave and that's what he did, at top speed. We bolted down that cart track. My feet slipped from the stirrups, which then bounced hard against my legs. I was all over the place in the saddle, and the reins were wrenched out of my fingers and were flapping along Tim's neck. The only way I could hang on was by lying forward and wrapping my arms round Tim's neck, and as my hat had also been dislodged and was tipped over my eyes I didn't have much idea where I was going. There was a sort of blur of bushes and trees whizzing by and a lot of snorting and harrumphing noises from Tim and, all in all, I was pretty much resigned to falling off dramatically, breaking a few bones, and ending up in hospital – or worse. There wasn't the slightest chance of my controlling Tim, so I concentrated on staying on for as long as possible. I managed to squint forward under the hat brim, and there, in front of me was this massive five bar gate, and all I could think of was Captain soaring over the wall earlier. For the second time that afternoon, I squeezed my eyes tightly shut so as not to watch the disaster that I was about to experience... and, suddenly, Tim stopped. Just like that. Obviously he didn't care for jumping the gate any more than

I did. I shot forward onto his neck, but I didn't fall and, once everything was still, I allowed myself to slide gently to the ground and sat there by Tim, whose sides were flecked with sweat, wondering what to do next.

"Are you all right?" It was Mr. Butler, leaning over me anxiously. I smiled weakly and nodded. A moment later, all the others had caught up and were crowding around me.

"Wow, you were like greased lightning," said Rosie with awe in her voice, as Caroline squatted down next to me and gave me a comforting hug and said, "Sure you're OK?" I got up, feeling vaguely light-headed, and was confronted by Chris, grinning triumphantly and offering me a high five. Yes, I thought, *yes*, I did stay on and I didn't make a fool of myself and everyone seems happy about it – except Mike, who was standing at the back of the crowd, scowling.

"Well done," said Mr. Butler, looking quite cheerful again. "Not far now. We'll have to walk the ponies anyway, now, to cool them down. Single file on the road, please."

He opened the gate by leaning down from Captain, which looked really hard, and led the procession down a short track to a lane. Caroline stayed at the back to close the gate, and then rode just behind me. After five minutes of steady walking along the empty lane, we went around a corner. There, in front of us, was the farmhouse, sunlight glinting on its windows.

As we turned into the stable yard, I gave a long sigh of happiness.

"Good day?" asked Phil who seemed to have recovered from his bad mood.

"Awesome!" I said happily. "But I'm tapped out. Can we watch TV?"

"Not yet. You'll have to wait a bit."

We'd got into the yard now and were dismounting. I gave Tim a pat. "Why?" I said. "Oh, and where does Tim go?"

"Tim," replied Phil, "doesn't go anywhere you don't go

55

for about an hour. You've got to unsaddle him, take off the bridle and wash it, give him a rub down, and turn him out into the field. I'll show you. Then, if you're lucky and aren't given any other jobs, you might get that rest."

I groaned. "It's not fair," I grumbled. "I'm really tired after all that trotting, and we're supposed to be on vacation, aren't we?"

Mr. Butler, who had an uncanny way of always appearing at the wrong moment, overheard this.

"This might be a vacation for you, my girl," he said sternly, "but it's no vacation for Tim. He's worked hard today, and he's put up with a lot from you – you've jerked his mouth and bounced and kicked till he was completely fed up, but he hasn't complained, has he? The least you could do is to look after him a bit now."

I blushed fiery red. "Sorry," I mumbled.

Rosie came over as Mr. Butler turned away.

"You really specialize in opening your big mouth at the wrong moment, don't you?" she said. "There's nothing he hates worse than people moaning and complaining about looking after the ponies."

I opened my mouth to object and then thought better of it. "Can you show me what to do?" I asked instead, rather helplessly. "Phil said he would, but he's gone off somewhere, and I don't know where to start."

"I'll bring Twinkle over, and we'll do them together," said Rosie kindly. "It all sounds a lot more complicated than it is. The first thing is to tie Tim to the fence with his halter rope so he doesn't go anywhere."

I copied how she ran the stirrups up the leathers and then undid the girth. "Lift the saddle off as gently as you can," Rosie instructed. We carried the saddles over to the tack room. It seemed funny to be in there again; so much had happened since I'd gone in so nervously that morning.

We went back to the ponies and took off their bridles, but not the rope halters underneath. "Don't you remember what Mr. Butler said? Take that off and you could have an impossible job catching him tomorrow," said Rosie, when I started to fumble with the knots. "Those halters never come off, as far as we're concerned." My fingers were tired and achy after the long day. It took me ages to undo the bridle's fiddly straps and buckles – I was much slower than Rosie. We queued at the outside tap to wash the bits, which were damp and slimy from the ponies' mouths. After hanging the bridles up in the tack room, we each grabbed a brush from a big pile of grooming tools. Rosie showed me how to brush in circles following the line of the coat, removing the sweat and dust of the day. There seemed to be an awful lot of Tim as I worked my way around him, but it was quite satisfying to do, and towards the end he turned his velvety muzzle into my hand and whinnied gently as if to say thank you. He was so sweet!

"Nearly done," puffed Rosie, brushing energetically. "Just check that there's nothing caught in their hooves, and then we can turn them out."

She showed me how to run my hand gently down each leg in turn, past his knobby knees and down to his ankles, though Rosie called them fetlocks, so that Tim lifted his feet obediently and let me inspect them. I was surprised at how heavy they were. Underneath were his shoes, strips of iron shaped to fit and nailed in place. The idea of doing that to a live pony gave me the shivers, though I knew really that it didn't hurt them. A sharp stone was stuck awkwardly under the edge of one shoe and Rosie demonstrated how to get it out it with a special tool called a hoof pick.

"He may have been lame in the morning if you'd left that there," remarked Rosie. "Now, untie him and we'll take them to the paddock."

57

We were the last to finish, as I was so slow, and it was getting cold. We led the ponies across the yard and through the gate to a large field where all the others apart from Captain were gathered, heads down, munching hard.

"They're as hungry as us!" I said. Tim pushed me aside with his nose. I dropped the rope and he trotted past me eagerly, and then stopped to graze. Twinkle joined him. We closed the gate carefully and leaned on it, watching the contented ponies.

"It's been a funny day," mused Rosie.

"Why?"

"Well, all that stuff with Chris. He's been showing off ever since he got here, so I suppose I don't blame Mike for losing his temper, but it was all a bit over the top."

"I was quite scared," I admitted, "though I'd more or less forgotten about it until now."

"You may need to be," Rosie said seriously. "Helping Chris like you did wasn't exactly tactful. Maybe Mike'll forget."

"Do you know him? Is he always like this?"

"We only met on Sunday," answered Rosie, shrugging. "Like I said last night, there aren't many boys here usually – they don't think riding's cool. Chris and Mike didn't know each other before, I don't think. Chris got on Mike's nerves right from the start, on the train we took on Sunday."

"Who's Phil?"

"He's from Mike's school, too, but they hate each other. That's why he's trying to make friends with the rest of us."

"I see." I felt a glow of pleasure; it sounded as if Rosie accepted me as a friend. Then I remembered Kate and Ed.

"Shouldn't we go in and find your sister?"

Rosie stretched and yawned. "I'm *so* tired! And if I know anything about anything, you'll be so stiff tomorrow you'll wish you'd never been born. Make sure you get a bath tonight, before all the hot water goes. Yeah, I suppose I'd better see what Kate's doing, as if I didn't know. I bet she and Ed'll be going all lovey-dovey and boring in the common room."

We strolled back across the yard. It was quiet now, with just the jostling and champing of Captain, who'd been stabled, disturbing the late afternoon peace. The sun had sunk lower and was gilding the windows blindingly, and the air smelled sweet and fresh, with just a tinge of a horsy smell to make it nicer. I found myself thinking about Martha and my other friends at home, doing all the usual holiday things, wandering through the shopping center, meeting up in the park, going swimming. In my imagination I'd just drifted towards home when I found myself in the common room surrounded by familiar people, with the smell of supper wafting about. Any chance of homesickness was banished.

The evening passed quickly. Mrs. Butler organized karaoke after supper. Kate spent the whole evening next to Ed. Rosie tried to talk to her a few times, but Kate ignored her. I kept far away from Mike, who glowered at me now and then.

By 10 p.m., I was quite happy to sink into bed. Rosie was already half-asleep. Kate spent a while brushing her hair in front of the mirror before leaping into bed.

"Sounds like you had an eventful afternoon," she said to me. "Rosie told me how you helped Chris."

"It was nothing," I muttered. "What happened to you after you got so wet?"

"It wasn't far back here by road. Mr. Butler was a bit angry but once he left and we'd changed, we could spend the whole afternoon doing what we liked." She sighed blissfully. "So, we went for a walk...."

"Oh," I said; it sounded rather dull. Then, plucking up my courage – I didn't want to look silly – I said, "Kate, you don't think Mike will – well, *do* anything to me, do you?"

"What? Oh, after that thing with Chris? Ed says Mike's a bit of a bully, but it was Chris he was after, not you. I wouldn't be bothered about it. There's lots more interesting things to do here."

She sighed happily again, turned over, and soon her steady breathing showed she was asleep. I lay awake for a time. All sorts of impressions danced behind my closed eyelids – Tim's rough-coated, muscular neck, the wild splashing of the fight, Chris's expression when he took up Mike's challenge, the terror I'd felt during that uncontrolled flight through the woods – and the triumph of smooth, rhythmic trotting.

Chapter 6

I sat up and groaned. It was dark because the sky was a blanket of black cloud, and heavy rain was beating against the window with a vicious, slashing noise. Muscles that I didn't even know I had had suddenly, overnight, taken on a screaming life of their own. I flexed myself carefully to see where it hurt most. My shoulders were sore, and my fingers ached. My bottom felt bruised from so much bouncing, and my legs ached as if I'd run a marathon. And then there were the rubbed patches on my thighs where the leggings were too thin to protect my skin properly.

Rosie was lying on her side, reading. Kate was still asleep, a blissful smile on her face. As I looked, Rosie rolled over and grinned ruefully.

"Guess who she's dreaming about?" she said. "D'you think we'll ever be that way about boys?"

I smiled back, but then grimaced as I moved a leg.

"Stiff?" asked Rosie sympathetically.

I nodded.

"I was a bit yesterday morning, but it was worse the first time I came. Something to do with using those muscles for the first time, I suppose. Didn't you have a bath last night?"

"I tried to," I said, "but there was a line, and I was too tired to wait any longer."

"Go and have one now, before they all wake up," Rosie suggested.

It was 8 a.m. Everyone would have to get up in half an hour – perhaps a good soak in the tub would help. I got up slowly and carefully, yelping once or twice when an awkward movement annoyed an already protesting muscle, and hobbled across the room.

"I feel about 91," I announced, "and if I don't reappear, you'd better come and fish me out, 'cause I might be stuck in the bath."

I grabbed a towel and limped painfully down the corridor. The bath was blissful. The water was boiling hot, and I filled it deep and sank in gratefully. Gradually the heat licked over the soreness and eased it. Perhaps I might be able to walk normally again one day, maybe in a week or two. Relaxed and warm, I'd almost drifted back to sleep when there was the sound of hurried footsteps, someone banged on the door of the bathroom, and a delicious scent of frying bacon floated up from the kitchen.

It was still raining heavily as I got dressed. I put on jeans, but the side seams rubbed the sore patches on my legs so I'd have to wear the leggings again. And anyway, the instructions had said not to wear jeans, especially in the wet. By the time I was ready, Rosie and Kate had disappeared downstairs, and I followed them as fast as my aching legs would let me. Everyone else was already eating.

Mrs. Butler caught sight of me. "Come on now, sit down and hurry up," she said, sounding rather impatient. "That's twice you've been late getting down here. We'll have to be getting you an early alarm call."

I blushed. "Sorry," I muttered, slipping into my seat. "I was taking a bath."

"Sore muscles?" asked Jane, next to me. "Agony, isn't it?"

I smiled at her gratefully and grabbed a Weetabix before they all disappeared. I felt ravenous – which was surprising considering how little I'd done since a gigantic portion of chicken pie and mashed potatoes for supper. I sloshed milk and sugar into my bowl and ate fast. Mrs. Butler was passing around plates with bacon, fried eggs, and fried bread, and I didn't want to miss out. I pushed the empty cereal bowl away just in time to grab the last plate.

"You'll be getting indigestion at this rate," said Mrs. Butler, watching me critically. I blushed again. Why did I do everything wrong? I ate more slowly and took time to look around the table. Chris was sitting next to Mike, I noticed with surprise, talking enthusiastically to him. Mike caught me staring.

"Watch it, you," he said quietly enough not to attract Mrs. Butler's attention, but menacingly enough to send a shiver down my spine. I looked away rapidly, puzzled. How come he could be perfectly friendly with Chris now, but not with me?

Ed and Kate were engrossed in each other. Rosie was watching them with an irritated expression. Most of the others were busy eating and talking, but Phil, who was sitting at the far end of the table, was picking sullenly at his half-eaten breakfast. Mrs. Butler stopped by him.

"Something else you don't like?" she asked.

"It's all right," muttered Phil, "but it's not like home."

"Well, I'm afraid you'll just have to get used to it," she answered briskly. "Either that or go hungry. Hurry up now, all of you, there's the ponies to see to."

I looked at the rain, which was still slashing against the windows. "We're not going out in this, are we?"

Mr. Butler came into the room at that very moment and overheard. "We'll see," he said. "If it eases a little, yes, we'll go. You're not afraid of a little drizzle, are you? But there's still plenty to do. Tack can be polished really well on wet mornings."

So, after breakfast, we all sloshed across the streaming

63

stable yard to the tack room and argued over saddle soap, metal polish, and where to sit. I watched carefully where Mike went, and found a corner well away from him. Phil came over and lowered himself to the ground next to me.

"Sore?" he asked.

"You bet," I answered, "and I'll be even sorer after all this polishing. It seems a bit much, having to do all this when we've paid to go on a vacation."

"Old Butler would just say it's not the ponies' vacation," he replied ruefully. He fished a bag of sweets out of his jodhpurs pocket. "Want one?" I took one gratefully. Phil crammed half a dozen into his mouth at once.

"I'm starving," he explained. "I don't like the food here. At home, Mom cooks exactly what I like, and she gives me a packed lunch for school. That's one of the good things about being an only child, isn't it – not having to share your mother's attention with anyone else, well, except for Dad, and he's not around much. I'd really hate it if I had brothers or sisters, wouldn't you? All your things are just yours, and no one comes and spoils them, or borrows them, or argues with you. And, of course, if you want to come on a holiday like this, you can get it because they haven't anyone else to pay for."

I stared at him. Then I said, carefully, polishing the saddle with great concentration, "Well, I'm not actually an only child."

Phil stared back. "You said you were, yesterday. Either you are or you aren't."

"Does it really matter?" I was getting confused now. "I'm here, and I'm me."

"Yes it does," replied Phil, in an oddly bitter voice. "I trusted you because you said you didn't have any brothers or sisters. I thought we could be friends. What did you lie for?"

I took a deep breath. This was all getting a lot more complicated than I'd bargained for.

"I forgot," I said.

"Forgot?"

"Well, yes."

"Don't be so lame!" He sounded really angry, as if I'd done something evil. "No one could forget a thing like that. You've done it on purpose, to get at me."

I stared at me. "Look, I *was* an only child. For 12 years I was the only one, and the center of anything, just like you said, except we've never had much money. But last summer Mom had the twins."

"Twins!" said Phil, horrified. "That must have been terrible."

I thought for a moment before answering. "Yeah, I suppose it was," I said slowly. "But it's different now. They're part of my family, and I love them, even though they've changed everything."

Phil stared at me blankly.

"What's the matter?" I asked.

"Nothing," he said. "Nothing at all." And he got up, lifted the heavy saddle, and deliberately crossed the crowded tack room to join the group around Mike.

I carried on rubbing at an awkward dull spot on the saddle, thinking about Phil. He's so prickly, flaring up at me just because of a silly mistake, I thought. And he seems really spoiled. Then I found myself wondering, was I a bit like that before the twins came along?

"Wow, what did you say to him to make him like that?" Rosie plunked herself down next to me.

"He's got himself into a tizzy, that's all."

"What about?"

I hesitated, about to tell her how weird Phil had been. But I saw that he was watching me from the other side of the room, and I couldn't help feeling sorry for him, so I stayed quiet. Rosie launched into a fit about Kate.

"She's always like this nowadays. We used to be such good friends and now all she's interested in is whatever boy she's got her eye on. She's supposed to have a boyfriend at home but it doesn't stop her flirting with Ed. Just look at them."

They didn't seem to me to be doing anything very much. They were both vaguely polishing bits of tack, sitting next to each other in a corner, sometimes talking and sometimes not. I rather envied them – it looked a nice way to spend time, companionable and friendly and maybe a bit exciting, like when they'd looked at each other yesterday in the stream and you could feel a sort of electricity joining them. I could feel Phil looking at me, and I couldn't help wondering if there might have been going to be something like that between us. But I didn't want to upset Rosie, so I said, "Never mind, it's only for a week, and they'll probably get bored with each other in a day or two," and Rosie agreed and looked happier.

Mr. Butler burst into the room, cheerful and strong, and somehow restored the atmosphere to normal instantly.

"Well!" he said. "The rain's eased off but you'll all need jackets. Go and get ready and then catch the ponies, and we'll be off. There's a hay barn where we can have our lunch indoors; it'll be too wet to sit outside."

I followed the general stampede to collect coats and run over to the paddock. My legs were still stiff, and I'd only just realized how relieved I'd been at the prospect of no riding today. All the confidence I'd gained yesterday had flooded away, and I couldn't remember a thing. I found myself wondering if I might miss riding if I exaggerated my aches and pains a bit… This is stupid, I told myself. You came here to ride and now you're trying to get out of it! Pull yourself together!

In the paddock, the ponies had gathered under the trees at

one side, sheltering from the continuing drizzle. Tim was among them, his gray coat dark with rain. I approached him slowly, my hand extended and, to my delight, he didn't back away but came calmly up to me so that I could easily get hold of the rope halter and lead him in to the stable yard. I wasn't sorry to see several other ponies were being very hard to catch, especially Mike's.

I was saddling up when the sweating Mike led his pony by. I couldn't resist smiling privately – a bad move, since he noticed. He tied his pony up and then sauntered by me on his way to the tack room.

"Funny girl, aren't you?" he muttered as he passed. "You wait, you won't be so happy later on, you'll see."

Rosie, next to me, overheard.

"Don't be so melodramatic, Mike," she called. "Let's forget it and just have a good time."

Mike grunted but he said no more. My stomach had plummeted but I smiled gratefully at Rosie, and resolved to keep well out of Mike's way for the rest of the day.

Before long, everyone was ready. Mr. Butler checked the gleaming tack and had a word of praise for me, as I'd remembered, just, how to put it all on Tim, with the odd word of help from Rosie.

"All mount!" he called, and very soon the procession was jangling along the damp lane in the opposite direction to the day before. Once in the saddle, I was pleased to find that my muscles protested less, and I concentrated hard on remembering all I'd learned yesterday. Tim seemed to respond to my growing confidence, and needed much less kicking to get him going. OK, it was still raining, and OK, I had a conflict ahead with Mike and I had no idea what was going on with Phil, but overall I felt a strong sense of pride and content.

Two hours later, it was much harder to remember we were on a vacation. The drizzle had turned back to rain once we were well away from the farmhouse – heavy penetrating rain that seeped down inside your collar and beat against your face. Drips fell at irritatingly irregular intervals from the brim of my riding hat, and my hands were frozen. Most of the others wore gloves; the only gloves I owned were at home. Every few seconds, I lifted one hand gingerly from my tight hold on Tim's saddle and blew hard against it, but the relief never lasted long. My thin leggings were soaked, with water running down inside my boots and, worst of all, as I lifted myself slightly in the saddle, the cold water spread under my bottom like an iced jelly. We plodded on dispiritedly in a long dreary line behind Mr. Butler. I was, as usual, at the end, but not quite, as Mr. Butler had told Caroline to stay behind me and make sure I didn't get left behind. I could see that this made sense, but it didn't stop me from feeling humiliated in front of the others.

The route led us up and over steep hilly paths, but the sheets of lashing rain obscured any views. Lulled into a sort of nightmare doze, I nearly swayed off Tim once or twice, saved, ignominiously, by Caroline's alertness.

I'd more or less decided that the ride would go on and on as miserably forever, when the line suddenly swerved to the right, and a stone barn, its great wooden doors open, loomed up through the rain.

Mr. Butler was annoyingly cheerful as he led us along. He told us to spread out our soaked coats to dry. Then the ponies were unsaddled and tied up in a line along the wall, and had to be rubbed down before they could be left, so he organized us to gather hay from the great bales at the other end of the barn and use it to make wisps to wipe some of the wetness from the ponies' coats. Tim insisted on eating his. By the time we'd finished, I'd warmed up, but I was still damp all over, and the thought of more hours of riding through the rain made me want to cry.

No one else looked much happier. We ate lunch huddled miserably by the hay bales, grateful for their scented warmth.

"Do we have to continue on this afternoon, Mr. Butler?" asked Rachel.

Several others joined in.

"It's so wet...I'm sure it's not good for the ponies. I suppose you couldn't organize a coach back, and we'd pick up the ponies later?"

Mr. Butler looked around at us.

"What a bunch!" he commented. "You'll survive, see if you don't. It's only been a bit of an April shower; you should see the weather here in the winter."

"No thanks," someone muttered.

"Anyway, it's brightening up out there," Mr. Butler went on, "so we'll have a good dry ride this afternoon."

"You said it was brightening up this morning," grumbled Kate. Chris got up and went over to the half-open doors.

"It is, you know," he called back. "The rain's nearly stopped, and there's some blue sky over there."

"Enough to make a sailor a pair of trousers?" asked Rachel, brightly. "That's what my grandma always says."

Ed pulled Kate up and they joined Chris at the doors.

"It'd have to be a pretty small sailor," remarked Ed. "But it's true – it really is clearing up."

By now almost everyone was crowding around the barn entrance. The wind was blowing the rain clouds away swiftly, and the heavy drumming of rain on the barn roof had given way to a gentler drip, drip, drip. Slivers of blue sky could be glimpsed between the racing clouds.

I stepped outside to look around now the mists of rain had gone. The barn was near the top of a hill. Far in the distance, I could see the huddled gray buildings of a village, but apart from that there was barely a trace of people. I drank in the

69

clean, sweet, moist air with relish. The scents were of mingled wet grass, hay, damp ponies, and a kind of indefinable open-air smell, infinitely nicer than the slightly sour street-smell at home. Half in a dream, I wandered across the paved area in front of the barn, my eyes fixed on the distant views.

"Having a good time?" asked a voice, smoothly. It was Mike. I felt a twinge of nervousness but tried to answer naturally.

"Yes, it's great here."

"Even better around the corner," he suggested. "Come and look."

He smiled sweetly, and I felt reassured. He must be trying to be friendly, I thought. I followed him round to the back of the big barn, and stopped, disappointed.

"There's nothing here." But I'd hardly looked back around at Mike before I felt myself being shoved forwards.

I was spread-eagled on the most disgusting pile of muck. The center of it, where my face had landed, was strong-smelling but fairly dry, but the edges, where my hands and legs were, were a revolting mess of filthy stinking liquid swimming with nameless lumps. I screamed in anger and flailed madly to get upright. By the time I could look, Mike had disappeared, and the others had come to see what was going on.

Phil and Rosie ran over to help me as Mr. Butler arrived.

"Oh no!" he groaned. "Not another crisis. I've never ever had a group like you lot to deal with. It's just one problem after another. How on earth did you manage to get there?"

I opened my mouth to explain and then shut it. Maybe, I thought, if I didn't tell on Mike, he'd consider he'd had his revenge, and leave me alone. If I made a fuss, it'd be my word against his, I'd look stupid and no one would want to be friendly any more. So I gritted my teeth and lied.

"It was all my fault. I went exploring and I slipped. Sorry."

"Yes, well, initiative is one thing, but this goes too far. Wash your hands in that water trough and then get inside and rub the worst off you with some hay. At least the sun's coming out, and you'll get dry fairly soon. And the rest of you, get those ponies ready and we'll be off."

A few moments later, Mr. Butler came up to me where I was scrubbing my legs with lumps of hay.

"You're quite sure it wasn't anyone else's fault?" he asked. "You're not hiding anything?"

I looked him straight in the eyes. "Not a thing; I was just silly," I said.

"Fair enough. I reckon you've punished yourself, so we'll say no more about it. Get Tim ready."

But when I got to the other end of the barn, I was surprised to see Tim already saddled.

"Mike did it," said Rosie, looking rather puzzled. "Are you all right?"

"Yes, fine," I said. I felt triumphant inside. OK, I had an unpleasant experience, but my theory about Mike must have been right. He was going to be nice to me from now on. I mounted quite easily by getting on to a hay bale first so I didn't have to stretch my protesting leg muscles and gathered the reins.

Rosie still looked puzzled. "You stink," she commented. "How on earth could you fall into a dung heap without noticing it?"

"I wasn't thinking," I answered airily, and kicked Tim on.

The sun was now shining quite warmly and made the damp ponies steam. I managed to get further forward in the line, and despite the horrible weather all morning I'd had time to get a lot more confident about riding. The route took us downhill for quite a long time, and then a wide grassy valley lay ahead invitingly.

"Let's all warm up with a trot," said Mr. Butler. "Kick on, everyone!"

I didn't have time to get nervous; Tim automatically followed the others into a fast, bumpy trot. I grabbed hold of the saddle to keep in it and tried to remember the rhythm of yesterday's trot. It eluded me for some time, while everyone else was apparently having no trouble at all, and I began to feel really annoyed with myself, and with Tim. Then, Mr. Butler cantered back and swung Captain around next to me.

"Just slow down a bit," he advised. "Then you'll get the timing."

So I consciously sat a bit longer at each bump in the saddle and then allowed myself to be jerked up and, all of a sudden, the magically sweet, easy movement returned. Tim carried on trotting gamely, I rose and fell in the saddle with no discomfort except for slightly tired leg muscles, and I even let go of the saddle and found I wasn't insecure.

"Terrific!" said Mr. Butler, approvingly. "You're doing very well. Keep it up!"

I glowed with pride as he kicked Captain on. The horse easily trotted past the ponies on his long legs till Mr. Butler reached the head of the line. He led us, still at a trot, away from the valley up the side of a long, sloping hill. It was harder to keep going, and the ponies gradually subsided back into a bouncy, uneven walk. Just as I was adjusting to the different feel, I felt myself sliding sideways. One stirrup was suddenly lower than the other and getting lower every second. A final awkward bounce from Tim was the last straw – the saddle skidded across Tim's back, I slid with it, and in an instant I was lying in a heap on the ground, one foot still tangled in a stirrup, and the saddle hanging half-loose under Tim.

Chapter 7

"Grab that pony!" yelled Mr. Butler.

Phil wheeled Bramble neatly towards me and grabbed Tim's dangling reins. Tim, who'd been standing stock still since I fell, moved restlessly at all this. My foot was trapped in the stirrup, and I could see his hooves, their iron shoes glinting, dangerously near. He moved a couple of steps forward, dragging me with him. I huddled in a ball, to keep well clear of those feet. Then, Caroline had jumped off her pony and was holding Tim securely by the noseband, and others were helping me disentangle myself.

"It's you again, isn't it," groaned Mr. Butler, as he pushed through the crowd. "All right?"

I nodded. I still felt shaken at the thought of the damage Tim's hooves could've done, but I wasn't hurt. Mr. Butler examined Tim's saddle.

"This wasn't done up properly," he said sternly. "That's why you fell. The buckle's been fastened a good three holes too loosely, so when you went uphill, it just swiveled off. That was your own fault, Jessica. I warned you yesterday that you can't have it too loose – just two fingers inside the girth, do you remember?"

"Yes, Mr. Butler. Sorry." I seemed to be spending a lot of time saying that. I fastened the girth buckle, and checked it was tight, and then remounted. Tim seemed quite all right, and I wasn't going to make a fuss now. But later – later, I'd have something to say to Mike.

The rest of the ride passed without incident. I felt fine about walking and not too bad about trotting, which we only did for short bursts. I was seething inside whenever I thought about Mike, but I had no intention of letting anyone see I was upset.

When we got back to the farmhouse, it took forever to groom the ponies – their legs were covered in mud. By the time we got indoors I was shattered. Upstairs in our room, I peeled off my leggings, which were stiff with dried muck and smelled disgusting, and left them in a heap on the floor. I wrapped myself in my towel and went to run a bath. While I was waiting for the bath to fill, there was a knock at the door.

"Who is it?"

"Me, Rosie. I've got some bath oil."

Rosie was looking worried when I opened the door. "Is there anything I can do to help?"

I gave a bright smile. "I can scrub my own back, but thanks for the oil. I do smell awful."

"Yes, but that wasn't what I meant," persisted Rosie. "I'm sure there's something wrong..."

"I'm fine." I took the bottle and half-pushed Rosie out of the room. "Just a bit stiff – and smelly!"

Rosie smiled, though her eyes looked puzzled. Then she shrugged, said, "See you for snacks then," and went.

After the bath, I felt better. I took the leggings down to Mrs. Butler, who was in the kitchen surrounded by steaming saucepans.

"My goodness, you've been in the wars!" she said, examining them. "I'll get them washed. Do you have anything else to wear?"

"Yes, these jeans."

Mrs. Butler looked doubtful. "We really prefer you not to wear jeans. If it rains again, they'll be very uncomfortable. Don't worry, I'll get them dry in time for tomorrow. Off you go, now. Supper's nearly ready. We don't want you being late again, do we?"

In the common room, everyone was gathered eagerly, all starving after the long day. I gravitated towards the other girls and kept well away from Mike. Soon we were eating huge platefuls of spaghetti and meatballs.

"Just the thing, after a day in the open air," said Mr. Butler. "Everyone warm and full now?"

There was a general murmur of assent, although Phil had, as usual, only picked at his meal. After his outburst that morning I'd hardly spoken to him, but in the common room, I went over to where he was sitting with his nose in a book.

"Thanks for helping when I fell off this afternoon. You ride really well."

"That's OK." He looked marginally more cheerful.

I didn't know what to say next but I wanted to be friendly, so I said, "How's things?"

"Why do you want to know?"

"Why shouldn't I?"

Phil looked up and shrugged. "OK, I suppose. I'm hungry, though."

I suddenly remembered that Mom had packed some biscuits in case I didn't like the food.

"Let's take them outside," Phil said. "I hate all this crowd in here."

I collected the biscuits and joined Phil leaning on the paddock rails, watching the ponies grazing. It was quite dark, but enough light came from the farmhouse windows to see their shapes as they moved slowly around. The only sounds were of grass being torn up and munched, and the occasional muffled thud of a hoof on the soft grass.

76

Phil accepted a biscuit but still looked at me in a funny way.

"Look, I'm sorry I upset you," I began. "It's really true that I forgot about my brother and sister – why should I say anything else?"

"That's not the point," he answered, moodily. "I thought you'd understand how I feel and you don't."

I thought about this for a minute. Then I offered Phil another biscuit. "Maybe you should tell me how you feel and then I'll tell you if I understand," I suggested.

He ate the biscuit moodily.

"The main trouble is, I don't get along with the others. They're all such good friends, and then there'll be a fight or an argument, and then they're all friends again. It doesn't make sense."

"Don't you know most of the boys from school anyway?"

"Not that well. We only moved after Christmas. I've never had any really close friends, anyway. Mom and I spend a lot of time together; that's usually better than being with a lot of silly kids."

I stifled a protest and said, "What about your dad?"

"He's away on business a lot. He's OK, but I don't see him much."

"So you and your Mom sort of rely on each other?"

"Yes. Ever since I've been old enough to help her and be a sort of companion to her. And she's really kind and loving – like cooking all the meals I like, for instance."

I watched the dark shapes in the field and tried to picture Phil's home life. "Why did you come here, then?" I asked.

"Oh, I don't know. The others were talking about it. It sounded a good time, and I like riding." Phil kicked a stone petulantly, and it bounced against the fence with a dull thud. "Well?" he demanded. "You said you could help me fit in. What about it?"

"Oh, Phil." I was almost laughing at the impossibility of it

78

all. "I can't sort out your problems, not like that. The only thing I've found out is that having to share your mom and dad isn't all bad. That's all."

"Thanks for nothing, you're just like all the rest," Phil sounded really fed-up. "No one understands."

He looked at me for a moment but I couldn't think what to say, so I just stared back rather hopelessly. Then he shrugged and went back to the house. I stayed where I was. I heard the door shut behind him as he went indoors and still I stayed there, leaning on the paddock railings, thinking hard. Up until this week, everything had always seemed so straightforward and simple; even not wanting the twins had seemed fair enough. I found myself disliking Phil's selfishness – he hadn't even talked about *my* feelings – and I wondered if I'd been a bit like that when it was just me, Mom, and Dad. That started me thinking of home and, to my surprise, I realized pictures of home always included the twins now, and that I didn't mind anymore. I even wondered if they might want me to teach them to ride one day.

Thinking about riding brought me back to Mike. I was still sore from falling and angry, too. It was unfair to pick on me when all I'd done was to help Chris. And what really puzzled me was that Mike had now apparently decided to be friends with him, but still hated me. I shook my head in bewilderment. It was all too much to work out; if only Mom was here to discuss it all. My eyes filled with tears. A few moments ago, my thoughts of home had been happy, but now a huge wave of homesickness broke over me and settled, swirling around me.

Gazing with tear-blurred eyes into the murky distance, I didn't notice anyone till a hand touched my shoulder and made me jump.

"Jess, what's the matter?" It was Rosie, kind and smiling and freckly faced.

79

I rubbed my eyes hastily with the back of my arm. "Nothing."

"Come on, I'm not stupid. Are you missing home? Or is there something else?"

I was glad I didn't have to lie. "I'm a bit homesick, yes."

"Well, that's no big deal," answered Rosie. "Everyone feels like that sometimes. It's nothing to be ashamed of. I've been lucky up till now 'cause Kate's been there but this time she might just as well be on another planet."

"I wish I could phone home."

"I know; I wish they didn't have that silly rule. Do you have a tissue?"

"No."

"Here you are. Wipe your eyes and blow your nose, and we'll sneak in quickly so no one sees you. Better?"

I nodded. Rosie took me by the arm and we crossed the shadowy stable yard back to the house, warm and safe with its glowing squares of window. Laughter and loud voices were coming from the common room, but Rosie hurried me past the half-closed door and up the stairs to our bedroom.

"Mrs. Butler's doing cocoa for everyone," Rosie said. "Shall I bring some up for us?"

"Would you? That'd be cool."

"No problem." The door shut behind her. I looked at my reflection in the mirror. It was a good thing Rosie had sneaked me upstairs. My eyes were red and my skin all blotchy. Mike would've noticed and make some nasty comment. Instead, Rosie and me could have a good gossip session over cocoa, and then go to bed when we were ready. I'd made a good friend, I thought; maybe we'd write to each other after the holiday. Maybe we could go and stay in each other's houses. Maybe we could even go riding with each other again!

Chapter 8

At breakfast next morning, Mr. Butler came in rubbing his hands.

"You'll be glad to know it's dried up for the day," he announced. "In fact, it looks like it'll be dry for the rest of the week."

There was a general cheer. The thought of another soaking wet ride hadn't appealed to anyone.

"Now, it's Thursday today," Mr. Butler continued, "in case anyone's lost track of time already. And the first thing we do today is ride to the nearest village so you can send a postcard home."

Matthew groaned. "That's boring. Do we have to?"

"Yes you do," said Mr. Butler, "I'll be checking up on you, too."

"What happens after that?" asked Rachel.

"We'll stop for a bit in the village in case you want to buy any souvenirs – so if you've brought any spending money, bring it today. Then we'll have a gentle ride to the high moor and have our picnic. This afternoon, we'll do some good hard riding and maybe a canter."

There was a murmur of pleasure from the good riders. I felt my stomach plummet to the ground.

"Then, tonight there'll be a quiz," Mr. Butler continued.

"And tomorrow?" asked Rachel again.

Mr. Butler chuckled. "You like everything mapped out, don't you? Tomorrow we have a ride out along a river valley and a bit of jumping for those who want to have a go. Then on Saturday morning there's a short ride, followed by a super–duper grooming and tack-cleaning session. Then we have a sort of end of week party, with gymkhana games in the paddock and a barbecue in the evening. And then, on Sunday morning, you're all off, and we get ready for the next group!"

"Any chance of a treasure hunt?" asked Chris. "I'm brilliant at those."

"I guess we could manage one," said Mr. Butler. "But that'll mean lots of leaping on and off the ponies, so you'd better practice your mounting."

"Oh, Chris is very good at mounting," said Mike, meaningfully, with a sly glance at me. Annoyingly, I blushed. I looked out of the window to avoid his stare.

"Everyone be ready to start in three-quarters of an hour, then," Mr. Butler announced.

There was a general clatter and bustle as mugs were drained and chairs pushed back. I still felt wobbly at the thought of all that difficult riding. Rosie came over.

"You'll be fine!" she said in a reassuring voice. "You're much better than you think you are. Come on, let's have a race to see who can get her pony ready faster."

Tim was tacked up and ready sooner than I would have thought it was possible two days ago. He whiffled his soft nose into the palm of my hand while I adjusted his noseband. His gentle brown eyes watched me trustfully as I moved round him, checking that the girth was properly tight. I lifted his feet up carefully, to examine them for any odd little stones which could cause him to go lame, and I admired the gloss on his coat, the product of my hard work with the grooming brush.

I was so absorbed, I jumped when Mr. Butler appeared at my side.

"Nice work," he said approvingly, inspecting Tim carefully. "You've taken a lot of care over him. Keep working at the riding, and you'll finish the week off a proper little horse-woman."

I glowed with pride. Rosie, not far off, flashed a smile across. Mike, on the other hand, was all too near. As Mr. Butler moved away, he came over.

"Who's a goody-two-shoes, then? Teacher's pet!"

I went red and felt tongue-tied. If only I could think of a way of answering back that might stop Mike from having a go at me whenever he could.

Without any warning he lifted his riding crop and flicked it towards my face threateningly. I couldn't stop myself from gasping, I really thought he was going to hit me, and he laughed nastily. I got together what courage I could find and pushed past, but just at that moment he lowered the stick, and it caught my leg. It stung so unbearably for a moment that I screamed. Several ponies, including Tim, reacted to the noise by stamping and swerving. Mr. Butler swung round from where he'd been talking to Kate.

"What the... What's going on?" he shouted.

"Sorry, Mr. Butler, I just flicked the crop as I walked by and it must've touched Jess," said Mike innocently. "An accident. It wasn't much."

My leg felt as if it had been burnt. Rosie looked furious, ready to burst into accusations, but I shook my head at her quickly.

"I'm sorry too," I said meekly. "It didn't really hurt. I shouldn't have screamed."

"I should think not. Scaring the ponies. No more silliness now. Everyone mount."

I quieted Tim and now stood facing his left side, ready to

83

mount. It was fairly easy now to reach the stirrup with my left foot and then to jump off my other foot and swing myself into the saddle. My leg still hurt, but I could ignore it. I wasn't going to be beaten by Mike, I just hadn't worked out the best way of beating him yet. I worked my right foot into the stirrup and leaned over to check the girth once more.

Rosie came clattering across the yard on Twinkle. "What's going on with you and Mike?" she demanded. "Why didn't you tell Butler the truth? I saw what happened – he didn't mean to hurt you, maybe, but he certainly wanted to frighten you. And there was something odd yesterday, too. Go on, let me help – I'm your friend."

I wasn't going to be able to keep all this to myself much longer. "I'll tell you later, when we get a chance to be on our own," I said hastily. "My leg's OK, just a bit sore. But I'm going to deal with this problem without grown-ups."

"You can count on me," said Rosie stoutly. "Forget all about it for now and enjoy the ride. We'll talk this evening."

She kicked her pony into line not far behind Mr. Butler, and I followed. We walked steadily out of the stable yard and down the lane. It was a fantastic morning for riding. The sun was sparkling on yesterday's raindrops, which still hung in the hedges. I could feel its gentle heat warming my shoulders through my sweater. Primroses and daffodils were clustered along the verge, in bright clumps of gold and green. Birds were everywhere, flying anxiously from place to place collecting food for their babies, who chirped piercingly from nests concealed in every hedge. Tim clopped along steadily and happily, not bothered by silly human quarrels. The lovely horsy smell of pony and leather and open air filled me with happiness despite everything.

"Trot on!" called Mr. Butler from the head of the line, and the ponies obediently broke into a trot, following their leader before we had a chance to give them the proper aids. I was

85

caught slightly off-balance and lost a stirrup. For a few moments of panic I felt sure I was going to fall off sideways, but I shortened the reins and got my footing back, got the bouncy rhythm right, and then I was trotting along as well as anyone else.

Several cars came past, mostly crawling so as not to disturb the horses. One came shooting past much too fast, and made some of the ponies skitter about. But my sensible Tim took no notice, and just went on with his fast clip-clop pace, while I rose and fell in the saddle just like a proper rider.

By the time Mr. Butler drew Captain back to a walk, we'd been trotting for about a mile and the line had spread out some way behind, as some of the ponies refused to trot all the time. Mr. Butler tut-tutted with irritation and called to everyone to stop while the stragglers caught up. It seemed ages till the last two came ambling into view. It was Kate and Ed, deep in conversation.

"Are you two riding or having a good talk?" bellowed Mr. Butler. Kate and Ed looked embarrassed as they gathered up long reins and urged their ponies forward to join the line. Rosie looked smug.

"Now you've finally decided to join us," Mr. Butler went on sarcastically, "we'll ride on to the village, where we'll tie the ponies up on the green. No one, I repeat no one, may leave his or her pony till I've checked they're properly tied up. We don't want any strays wandering about the roads causing accidents. Then you'll have an hour to look around and buy your souvenirs and postcards. Don't forget stamps. If anyone needs a pen, I've brought plenty. All right?"

There was a general murmur of assent. Mr. Butler turned in the saddle to the front again and urged Captain back into a trot. We trotted for ages, but this time I was ready and felt balanced right from the start, though my legs were really tired by the time we reached the village. I felt incredibly proud as we clattered along the street, with people smiling and waving at us.

The green was wide and grassy with a post and rail fence along one side where the ponies had to be tethered. Mr. Butler and Caroline checked the knots carefully, and then we were free to explore the shops.

"What are you going to buy?" I asked Rosie.

"Something nice for Mom and Dad," she replied, "and something nice for me. And a postcard, of course."

I smiled but I felt ill at ease again. Why was I always the odd one out?

"How about you?" Rosie was asking.

"I suppose I'll try and get something for Mom and Dad and something for the twins but I don't have much money. Hardly any at all, in fact. I didn't know we were supposed to bring spending money."

"Why don't we choose the postcards and go on from there?"

There were two racks of postcards. There were some ordinary views of the countryside, some bigger, very glossy cards, and right at the bottom, some pictures of ponies grazing.

"Are these tattered pony ones the same price as the others?" asked Rosie, cleverly.

The man leaned over the counter. "I'd forgotten those old ones. They're half price. Old stock."

I smiled at Rosie gratefully and chose two cards showing a gray pony like Tim, one for Mom and Dad and the twins, and one for Martha. The souvenirs were much too expensive. Rosie picked out a little china pony for herself, a tea towel for her mother, and a pen for her father, and she'd probably still have some change. It wasn't fair.

Rosie paid and joined me as I wandered around disconsolately, torturing myself by looking at all the lovely things I'd like but couldn't afford.

"Why don't you just buy the postcards?" she suggested. "This isn't the only shop, and we have plenty of time."

"Good idea," I said, cheering up. We wandered around the green, where Caroline was sitting on a bench near the ponies eating doughnuts, but all the shops had the same sort of goods at the same sort of prices. Mike and his gang were in one shop – Chris was talking loudly – so we avoided that one. I was beginning to think I'd better forget the whole idea of souvenirs when Rosie grabbed my arm and dragged me down a narrow alleyway to a dusty little shop, which looked apologetic, nestled up against the smart tourist traps.

The old woman knitting behind the counter was the only person there.

"Can I help you, girl?" she asked. Her face was wrinkled and warty like a witch from a children's story.

"I'm looking for presents to take home, but they have to be very cheap. They are for my parents, and I have a baby brother and sister."

The woman gave a sudden cackly laugh.

"I've got the very thing here somewhere," she said. She disappeared behind the counter. Leaning over, we could see her delving deep into a pile of cardboard boxes. Dust blew up in clouds. We had to jump back suddenly when she straightened unexpectedly and held out two slim plastic tubes, one red and one blue.

"Bubbles," she said. "Babies love bubbles. I've had 'em for donkey's years. I'll be glad to see the back of 'em. There's not much call for bubbles round here."

Rosie gave a spurting giggle and turned to look out through the grimy window, her shoulders heaving.

"Your friend all right?" asked the woman.

"Yes she's fine," I answered, struggling to keep a straight face myself. "Just hiccups."

"You want some water then, girl?"

"No thanks, no. Er, you said you might have something I could give my Mom and Dad?"

The old woman promptly disappeared behind the counter again, like a reverse jack in the box. We clung together in mounting hysteria and stuffed our hands into our mouths to stop the sound of giggling. She was gone for ages this time but we didn't dare look over the counter in case we met her coming up. We'd just got ourselves a bit more under control when she popped up again.

"You cast your eyes over this lot," she urged. "Fit for a king, this stuff."

She had brought up a card of plastic jewelry, packets of hairnets, a ratty plastic handbag, and an assortment of other things. I looked at them with disappointment.

"I don't think there's anything..." I started, but Rosie, giggles forgotten, was rummaging through the pile.

"What about this? And this?"

She'd unearthed a tiny pottery brooch with a delicately modeled daffodil glowing golden against a white background, and a maroon key case. I was thrilled.

"They're just right! How much are they?"

"How much do you have?" asked the old woman.

"Not very much." I dug in my pocket and held out the collection of coins without much hope.

She gave her cackly laugh again.

"You're in luck, girl," she said. "That's exactly right, no more, no less. I'll put the bits and pieces in a bag for you, shall I?"

Everyone had assembled on the green, perched precariously on the fence or squashed together on the benches, writing postcards and sharing sweets, except for Phil who was sitting all alone eating a chocolate cake. I wrote:

Dear Mom and Dad and Tim and Holly,
Having a brilliant time. We go riding every day, even in the rain, and my pony's named Tim – isn't that weird? There's a cool girl here named Rosie who's my best friend. We share a room with her sister Kate – she's nice too. I can trot already and soon I'll be cantering. I fell off but it didn't hurt and it wasn't Tim's fault.

See you on Sunday,
Lots and lots of love, Jess X X X

The one to Martha was more or less the same but I left out the bit about Rosie in case she minded.

Rosie went to talk to Kate who was, as usual, engrossed with Ed, eating crisps and sharing his headphones to listen to music together. She came back a few moments later, muttering crossly about Kate being obsessed.

Mr. Butler went around collecting cards and checking everyone had written one. He sent Caroline over to the post box on the other side of the green, and told everyone else to get ready to ride on and, before long, we were clattering along the street again in a long, happy line.

Chapter 9

We had lunch sitting on an outcrop of rocks high in the hills. The breeze was cold and no one wanted to linger there. I wished yet again that I brought some gloves as we got the ponies ready for the afternoon's ride. But I'd managed to avoid Mike all morning, and Phil seemed to be avoiding me, so, apart from cold hands, I was OK. There wasn't a chance for Rosie and me to talk about the Mike situation in private and, anyway, I was getting a bit fed up with her continual digs at Kate.

It all came to a head soon after we set off again. Rosie and me were talking about school, and Rosie called over to her sister.

"Kate, what's the name of that science teacher you used to have, the one you hated?"

Kate, riding alongside Ed, apparently didn't hear.

"Kate! I'm talking to you!"

Kate glanced back dismissively. "Shut up, Rosie. I'm busy."

"Kate! Don't be such a jerk! Tell me!"

Rosie was getting really heated, and I was embarrassed.

"It doesn't matter, Rosie."

"It does."

Rosie kicked Twinkle on so that she pushed in between Kate and Ed.

"What's the matter with you?" she demanded. "Have you gone deaf or something?"

Kate lifted an eyebrow disdainfully. "I'm just not very interested," she replied coolly. "Ed and I are having an adult conversation."

"Oh yeah?" said Rosie sarcastically. "Well, you might be all wrapped up in Ed, but I'm still your sister and we've always had time for each other, so there's no need to change just because of some stupid boy. And, anyway I'll tell Mom about everything, and then..."

"Get lost," interrupted Kate.

Rosie stuck her tongue out at her.

"For God's sake, Rosie," Kate said, "just leave us alone."

"No."

"Well, in that case I'll make you."

Kate leaned over and hit Twinkle hard on the flank. She broke instantly in a canter. Rosie grabbed her mane as they shot past everyone else. Several other ponies thought things were livening up and started to canter too. I pulled on Tim's reins as hard as possible and prayed he wouldn't join in.

"Everyone stop!" yelled Mr. Butler.

Most people did but Rosie, Adam, and Matthew were all ahead by now and none of their ponies wanted to stop. Caroline pushed Micky past us and, once she was clear, kicked him on to a fast canter while Mr. Butler blocked the way for the rest of us. Caroline quickly caught up with Adam, whose pony was quite small and hadn't kept up, and helped him rein her in. Rosie managed to pull Twinkle back to a walk and turned him to come back, but Matthew's pony careered into the distance with Matthew bouncing around wildly and his stirrups flying. A few seconds later he lost the battle to stay on and landed on the ground with a thump. Irritatingly, his pony decided at that moment that he'd had enough and stopped just beyond.

Caroline was off Micky in a flash and down on her knees next to Matthew. A second later, he stood up.

"He's OK," she called back to us. "No damage this time."

"On!" called Mr. Butler.

The ride continued. Kate rode as close to Ed as she could, her stirrups brushing against his, talking to him in a low voice. He wasn't looking particularly happy any more. Next to me near the back of the column, Rosie muttered rude remarks about Kate non-stop. I found it all very awkward. I liked Rosie, but Kate was all right too, even if she was a bit obsessive about Ed, and Rosie really had been unnecessarily touchy. I mean, there's nothing surprising about a couple of 14 year olds getting together, is there? After a while Rosie calmed down, so I ventured, "All right now?"

"I'll survive. But that sister of mine won't. She's such a pain, and I don't see why she should get away with it. I really hate her when she's like this."

I shrugged and kept out of it. We rode along moorland tracks for an hour or so, mostly trotting although we gave the ponies a breather sometimes by letting them walk. I practiced taking my feet out of the stirrups and letting them dangle, which is what most of the better riders did a lot. It was easy when we were walking but trotting like that's more difficult. You have to sit well down into the saddle and let yourself bounce gently with the pony – it made me feel my teeth rattling – but the really good thing is I never felt I'd fall off.

Eventually we got to a stream where we had to dismount and let the ponies drink. Rosie deliberately barged past Kate and let Twinkle drink where she'd been going to go. Kate looked daggers at her and aimed a kick at her before taking her pony further downstream. I noticed Ed had joined Mike and Chris. Phil, who I'd hardly seen that day, pulled Bramble over to join me and gave me a bit of chocolate.

"Lovely, family life, isn't it?" he said sarcastically, watching Kate and Rosie. "I bet you're looking forward to seeing your brother and sister again. Think of all the fun you'll have together."

"It's not all like this," I said. "Kate and Rosie are best friends most of the time."

"Oh yeah?"

At that moment, Kate sauntered past Rosie and deliberately stuck out a foot and tripped her up. Rosie let out a howl as she landed on the peaty grass.

"Now I'm all wet, you horrible beast!" she screamed. "This grass is soaking. You wait till I get my hands on you!"

She jumped up and grabbed her sister's ponytail. Kate screeched. She twisted round, pulled Rosie's hands away, and slapped her face. Rosie screamed dramatically and reached out to thump Kate back, but at that moment Mr. Butler pushed his bulk between them and pulled them apart so that, panting angrily, they stared at each other a few feet apart.

"That is quite enough from both of you!" snapped Mr. Butler. "Get back on your ponies! This is your last warning – any more behavior like this and you'll be sent straight home. If you can't behave in a civilized manner, you'd better keep well away from each other for the rest of the ride."

Both girls looked livid but they remounted sulkily and Kate was told to go to the front with Mr. Butler and Rosie to the back with Caroline – and me.

Mr. Butler led us along the stream until the path opened out into a lush valley with farm buildings at the end.

"We'll have a canter here," he said. "Anyone not happy?"

I put up my hand instantly. So did Adam and Jane and Matthew.

The rest were told to trot first, then canter up to the buildings. Then they could regroup and come back towards us at a canter again.

"Watch carefully," Mr. Butler advised us beginners. "See how they apply the relevant aids. It's not very hard. Then you can have a try."

A day or two ago, I'd have been totally terrified at the prospect, but my confidence had been growing without my realizing it. The better riders kicked from a walk into a trot. Then, for a moment, they seemed to be bouncing instead of rising, like I'd done when I started trotting, and then suddenly the ponies' pace changed and they were shooting off into the distance. At the farm buildings, they all stopped and waited till everyone was ready, before flying back to the start again. Most of the riders looked exhilarated, though one or two, including Rosie, looked rather scared.

"So," said Mr. Butler, "What do you have to do to canter?"

Ed, who'd looked really expert, explained. "First, you get your pony to do a good fast trot. Then you do sitting trot, let your hands go forward, kick on, and there you are."

"It's miles easier cantering here than in the riding school at home," commented Rachel. "Why's that?"

"Partly because the ponies here are all cantering together," explained Mr. Butler. "It's more like play than work for them. The only danger comes when they start off unexpectedly – like they did earlier today. They're herd animals; they like doing the same as their friends. And then at home the pony has to be on the right leg for turning the corners, whereas here it doesn't matter which leg he's on as he's going straight ahead."

I was a bit flummoxed by all this talk about legs – surely the pony just took both legs in turn. Seeing my puzzled face, Mr. Butler explained how, in canter, a pony uses one front leg ahead of the other all the time, so that if there's a circular course, it's important to lead off with the inside leg or the pony will be unbalanced.

"The best practice is to do a figure of eight, so that you get the pony to change legs in the middle. But you don't need to bother about that for now," he said kindly. "Now, how about stopping? Mike, you tell us."

"Sit down firmly in the saddle and pull the reins," said Mike, sounding bored. "Easy except for total beginners who bounce around all over the place." He stuck his tongue out at me once Mr. Butler wasn't looking. I ignored him but inside I was furious. It wasn't my fault that I hadn't cantered before.

"Yes, but don't pull hard on the reins or you'll hurt the pony's mouth. A gentle tightening should be enough. And then?"

"Once the trot is established, you start rising again," said Kate.

"Quite right. I'm glad to see you've rejoined the civilized world," said Mr. Butler. From behind his back, Rosie made a face at her sister. "Now, how do you feel about having a try?" he asked me and the others.

"I'll try," I said, my heart thumping. The others nodded, except Matthew, who said he'd had enough cantering for one day and would stick to trotting, so he and Caroline went ahead to wait for us.

Mr. Butler organized us into three groups with a beginner in each.

"The ponies are quite tired," he said, "so they won't go that fast, and they'll stop by those buildings anyway."

I was in the second group. I watched the first group move into trot, and tried to remember all the things I'd been told, and to watch them happening. Jane was the beginner in the group. She looked very tense and held the reins tightly. As the other ponies extended their stride to a canter, she jerked back nervously, and her pony jiggled a bit and then reverted to a trot. She reached the farm buildings well after the others.

"See where she went wrong?" Mr. Butler asked us.

"Did she pull him back to a trot?" asked Adam.

"That's right. It's no good asking for a canter with your legs but for a walk with your arms. You've got to let the reins give a bit. Now then, Jess. Your turn."

I squeezed the placid Tim gently with my legs, and he joined the other waiting ponies. Their riders, Rob, Kate, and Rachel, all looked happy and excited. I patted Tim's warm gray neck nervously, hoping he wouldn't go too fast.

"Trot on!" said Mr. Butler.

We trotted almost immediately. The others moved rapidly into a canter, and I realized Tim had followed without my doing a thing. His sturdy legs pounded along the turf, his mane flying in the wind. His stride was smoother than at a trot, yet I seemed to be flung about in the saddle in a very uncontrolled way. It was brilliant but a bit scary. I grabbed hold of a piece of mane for extra balance and unintentionally pulled on the reins. Tim changed pace back to a trot and then stopped dead. The others had reached the buildings. I had to whack his sides hard to get him to walk the last few yards, feeling rather silly.

"Not at all bad," said Rob generously. "At least no one's fallen off yet."

He spoke too soon. The last group set off with enthusiastic whoops and went really fast. They jostled to an unruly halt when they reached us, and Rosie lost her stirrups, tried to hold on by hugging Twinkle's neck, but slithered off clumsily and landed with a thump. I heard Kate draw in her breath sharply, but as Rosie got to her feet unhurt, rubbing her bottom, Kate had already turned away and busied herself with something else.

Phil came off worst, as Bramble was always difficult, and reared as they halted, but Phil was certainly a good rider. Not only did he cling on, but he quickly calmed Bramble down, and walked her in circles till she'd settled.

The rest of the afternoon's ride passed in a happy blur as I dreamed about cantering. I'd done just enough to have a glimpse of why everyone else loved it so much, and I was dying to have another chance, but there wasn't a chance that day – we were soon onto a lane and, anyway, the ponies had to be allowed to cool down before we got back home.

Chapter 10

"Who wants to be in my team?

"Me!"

"Me!"

"Not me!"

It was time for the quiz. Before supper we'd had a massive game of tag. Rosie was totally preoccupied with Kate and Ed and seemed to have forgotten her promise to advise me about Mike. I got a sick feeling in my tummy every time I saw him, and kept waiting for him to do something horrible, but all he'd actually done was to tag me very hard. I decided to wake Rosie up early tomorrow and go out for a talk then.

Mr. Butler appointed Jane and Kate as the two team leaders.

"If I choose one boy and one girl," he said, "we'll have sexist teams, and that won't do."

"Not if Kate's got anything to do with it," remarked Rosie slyly.

"Well, the one person I don't want in my team is that fat squirt Rosie," announced Kate loudly. "You can have her, Jane."

"Let's choose one at a time," suggested Jane, looking embarrassed. "I'll have Rachel."

"And I'll have Ed," said Kate.

"What a surprise," said Rosie, loudly.

"Rosie," said Jane, with a sigh.

"Mike."

"Chris."

The choosing went on till only Phil and me were left. Jane and Kate looked at us speculatively. It was horrible being last, though I understood why; everyone knew I didn't know much about horses, and Phil's moodiness made him unpopular. I wished hard for Jane to pick me so I wouldn't have to be with Mike.

"Jess," said Jane. Phil joined Kate sulkily, muttering about how he hated team games.

"OK, if everyone's sorted out, we'll get started," announced Mr. Butler. "We'll start with a round of horsy questions, but there'll be other categories too. Only one person from each team can answer, and if you get the answer wrong, the other team has a try. Ready?"

The two teams all nodded. We were at opposite ends of the big common room with Mr. Butler in the middle. The first question was to Kate's team.

"What's the proper name for a horse that's black and white?"

Rob's hand shot up. "Piebald," he said.

"One point. Jane's team: Name three native breeds of pony."

"What do you mean – like New Forest?"

"Yes."

There was a pause before I shyly volunteered, "New Forest, Exmoor, and Shetland?"

"Quite right. Don't look so surprised, Jessica."

The round finished at a draw, 10 points each. The next section was about sport. Kate's team, all boys except her, were good at this and ended up eight points in the lead. We were better at the third round, about current affairs, and Kate's team finished only three points up.

"Half-time," said Mr. Butler. "There are drinks and biscuits on the table. We'll start again in 10 minutes."

Jane gathered us in a huddle. "Let's be cleverer and work out the answers together," she suggested. "I know only one person can answer but he didn't say we couldn't consult each other first. And that way we'll avoid throwing points away." She glared at Rosie who'd butted in two wrong answers in the sport round before anyone else had a chance to say anything, and Rosie had the grace to blush.

The next category was animals. We did OK, but Kate answered all the other team's questions before anyone else, made several mistakes, and gave us the chance for bonus marks.

"Books," announced Mr. Butler. A few groans came from the boys. The questions were all really old-fashioned and none of us except Kate knew things like the author of "Treasure Island," so her team got all the bonus points.

"We'll walk it," said Kate smugly. "We have two points in hand, and we've been in the lead most of the time. Lucky I knew all those book questions, wasn't it?"

The rest of her team looked annoyed, especially Ed who was carefully avoiding her. He'd been growing cooler all day. The other boys kept teasing him, and Kate's behavior must have put him off.

Anyway, our team was determined to fight. The last round was riding skills and we concentrated hard. I'd learned a lot during the last few days and actually knew the answers to questions like "Describe the aids needed to turn your pony a quarter circle," but I was careful not to say anything without checking with the rest.

By the last pair of questions, we were equal again.

"Final question," said Mr. Butler, "and it's the same for both teams." He handed out two outline drawings of the side view of a pony, and two pens.

"Oh, no, I can guess what's coming," moaned Rachel. She was right.

"You've got five minutes to name as many parts of the horse as you can, starting from now," announced Mr. Butler.

The two teams pored over the pictures, whispering for secrecy.

"Can we put down things like 'ear'?" I asked.

"Don't see why not," muttered Jane. "Let's do all the easy ones and then see what else we know."

She labeled busily while we watched and prompted.

"Let's hope spelling doesn't count," remarked Rosie after a while. "I'm sure some of these are wrong."

"Don't fuss," said Jane shortly. "OK, what else? How much time do we have left?"

Chris consulted his watch, which he never tired of telling us was full of gadgets. "Two minutes and thirty-two seconds," he said, "and you've forgotten 'fetlock'."

"Well, where is it?"

"Ankles," Rosie said.

"I thought it was that fringe bit between the ears," suggested Rachel.

"No, Rosie's right," said Chris.

Jane looked at the picture doubtfully. "Anyone else know?" There was silence.

"We'll go with the majority," she said, and drew a line from just above the pony's hoof and wrote "fetlock".

"Ponies have hocks, too, don't they?" I suggested. "But I don't know where."

"I do!" shrieked Rosie. "The hock's on the back leg, sort of halfway up."

"Sssh!" admonished the others, as Kate's group looked across, nodded to each other, and bent over their picture.

"Idiot," said Jane. "We'll never win if you shout them out like that."

Rosie made a face at Jane and withdrew from the group to sulk. I felt impatient with her; she'd been silly all day about Kate, and she might at least say she was sorry now.

"Of course, what we should do is to say the wrong words loudly and then the other group would copy and get them all wrong," suggested Chris mischievously.

Rachel and I giggled, but the others were disapproving.

"That'd be cheating," said Jane primly. "We'll win – or lose – fair and square."

"Have it your own way," said Chris airily, "but you realize there's only one minute left? How many do we have?"

"Sixteen," said Jane, after counting. "But I'm not sure they're all right. I've never even heard of a poll – except for a parrot. And I thought pasterns were gates to castles. I'm sure we learned about those in school."

"Well, let's hope we don't get minus marks if we're wrong," said Rachel. "I know, we forgot 'shoulder'. That's the part you pat in front of the saddle isn't it?"

"No," put in Matthew, "that's the withers. I think the shoulders are further down."

"Well, make your minds up!" urged Jane, scribbling over the first line and redrawing it below. "Any more ideas?"

No one had any. We sprawled round the picture in silence, staring at it, till Mr. Butler yelled, "Time's up!"

"Jane's team first," he said, producing a green felt tip pen to mark off the answers. "One point for a correct answer and one off for a mistake. Yes... yes...no... yes... oh, dear God, no!"

"What?" Rosie asked, craning to see.

"His flanks are his sides, not his neck," said Mr. Butler. "But you've got 'withers' right – well done. That's – 15 altogether. Added to your other marks, that puts you 15 in the lead. Let's see what the other group have produced."

He pulled out the other sheet from underneath. It looked

105

really impressive with loads of labels. Mr. Butler ticked and corrected in silence, and then looked up.

"Well, this group has some very, how shall I put it, original ideas," he announced. "I've certainly never heard of half of these. Whose idea were they?"

"Kate's," said Ed. "She said she knew them all."

"She said she's an expert," added Rob.

"They're not really wrong, are they?" asked Adam.

"They're not in any book I've ever read," said Mr. Butler. "You could, of course, argue that any self-respecting horse ought to have a winder spoon and a hoof cover – but I've never come across them. Oh, no, not this one either. Or this."

Kate looked down at her feet.

"You said you knew," said Mike accusingly. "And we were stupid enough to believe you."

"Show-off," remarked Ed witheringly. The other boys in the team just glared.

"Now then, that's enough," said Mr. Butler. "Let's see – you've got 16 right, but there's seven wrong, so that gives a total of nine, which makes Jane's team the overall winners. Well played everyone."

My team cheered and clapped and hit each other's backs with pride .

"Do we get a prize?" asked Chris eagerly.

"You certainly do." Mr. Butler gave each of us a giant bar of chocolate.

"Don't the others get anything?" I asked. I couldn't help feeling rather sorry for Kate, who was looking very uncomfortable.

"I'm glad you thought of them," said Mr. Butler. Behind him, Mike pulled a face and mouthed "creep" at me. "Yes, there are consolation prizes, too." The losers each got a smaller bar of chocolate.

"Bed," announced Mr. Butler at last. "And, though I'm not

trying to sound like your parents, tooth brushing is in order. It's not just the ponies who need grooming, you know."

We all smiled dutifully. Kate whispered something to Ed, but he didn't reply. As we went upstairs, Kate was ahead of us, back straight and head high, all alone.

I thought Kate and Rosie would have a big argument, but they didn't. Kate was very dignified as she undressed and got into bed, and turned her back on us to read.

Rosie made one or two snide remarks about show-offs and ignorant pigs, but as she got no response from Kate and no encouragement from me, she shrugged and gave up. In a few minutes they were both fast asleep. I lay awake, going over the day in my head. Most of it had been so wonderful. The memory of Mike hitting me filtered into my thoughts and I rubbed the bruise on my leg, but even that couldn't destroy the fun I'd had, or the fantastic thought that tomorrow, we'd be cantering again.

Chapter 11

There must be something in the theory that you can tell yourself to wake at a certain time, because I was wide awake at 6 a.m. on Friday morning and that would never ever happen at home, unless the twins are crying. Isn't it strange how for years you wake at the crack of dawn, and then suddenly go to the other extreme and want to sleep all morning? It confused my dad completely when it happened to me a couple of years ago, and he still gets moody on weekends when I'm not ready to get up at 8:30 a.m.

Anyway, Rosie and Kate were snoring in unison, and I felt quite mean waking Rosie, but there never seemed to be a moment during the day when you could guarantee a bit of privacy. I shook her gently and she groaned and grumbled a bit, and then when she woke up I reminded her that we needed to talk and she remembered and jumped out of bed.

So that we wouldn't wake Kate, we dressed in the bathroom, giggling a lot, and then we crept downstairs and let ourselves out. No one seems to lock doors in the country. The sun was already strong and we went to my favorite place, the paddock fence, and hoisted ourselves to sit on it, so we could look at the ponies, which were all clustered together under some trees, heads down to the grass.

"Eating breakfast," remarked Rosie. "Lucky things. We should have grabbed some food – I'm starving."

"I'll get us something." I jumped off the fence and went back to the farmhouse. I didn't want to get us into trouble, but there always seemed to be plenty of food about, so I grabbed some sliced bread and a couple of apples from the piled-up fruit bowl.

We munched for a while, feeding apple cores and bits of bread to the ponies that jostled round us once they noticed the food.

"OK, down to business," Rosie said through a mouthful. "Mike. He's had quite a few goes at you, hasn't he?"

"Umm. The worst was when he shoved me in that muck-heap. I felt so stupid letting him trick me like that and I smelled disgusting."

"You sure did. Well, we know why he started, when you made him look silly by helping Chris, and it looks to me like he's just having fun bullying you now. You know, he's doing just enough to make you scared and not enough to get caught out."

"Kate said that Ed said he's got a reputation for bullying people. So maybe he's picked on me because he likes having a victim."

"Well, it's up to us to get in his way," said Rosie stoutly. She jumped down, and paced up and down, thinking. "We need to give him a taste of his own medicine. That'll put him off. My father says that bullies are really cowards."

"I'm not sure I believe that," I said doubtfully. "Teachers and parents are obsessed with bullying, but they don't seem very good at actually stopping it. What if it just makes things worse?"

"I bet anything you like, if we make Mike look stupid, and you get even, he'll back right off. He's not evil. He may be quite pleased to have a chance to be friends."

I didn't exactly believe that, but it was a nice idea, and if Rosie was going to help I was ready to try some sort of revenge. The prospect made me feel sick with fear in case it made things worse instead of better, but there didn't seem to be much alternative. We talked for ages about what we could do. I didn't want to be drawn into hurting him or putting him into any sort of danger – it had to be something that would make everyone laugh at him, and he also had to know we'd engineered it. That's not as easy as you'd think. In the end, we agreed that we'd stick together during the morning ride and look for an opportunity.

By now, the others were up. Jane and Rachel joined us, and we talked ponies for a bit before going in to breakfast. Kate was eating cereal at one end of the table, looking sulky. Most of the boys, including Ed and Mike, were clustered at the other end, talking football. Phil joined us and discussed riding in a surprisingly cheerful manner, and even ate some sausage. He brought Bramble over to Tim and me while we were saddling up and chatted away as if we were best friends. Rosie looked as if she was going to giggle, but kept well away till we started off. Then she pushed Twinkle into line between us. Phil looked annoyed, but he couldn't do much about it, as Mr. Butler insisted the ponies always went in single file along the lanes and shouted at anyone who tried to overtake.

We went through a gate and followed a narrow track down and down and down, with woods on both sides. It was quite creepy – not the sort of place I'd ever want to be at night. Rosie looked back a few times to ask if I had any ideas for getting even with Mike, but nothing came to mind.

We came out of the woods into a wide valley that stretched ahead for miles. There was a river gleaming down the center, with green fields either side. There were cows and sheep everywhere, and every time we crossed into another field, there was a gate. Usually Caroline did the gates but she let a couple of the better riders have a try maneuvering their ponies around to hold the gate open and then the complicated business of shutting it again, all of course without dismounting. When she said Mike could try, I was last in the line. He opened the gate neatly, watched everyone ride past, smirked nastily at me as I went by, and then closed the gate so sharply behind me that it caught poor Tim's hocks. His natural reaction was to kick out, even though he was such a gentle, well-mannered pony, and it would have served Mike right if Tim had kicked him or Bilbo, but no such luck. What did happen was that I was caught completely off-balance and fell forward over Tim's shoulder. For a horrible long moment, I was completely breathless. Afterward, I wondered if that was what Kate and Rosie had been talking about when they described being winded. It didn't last long, and I wasn't hurt so I stood up and found, to my surprise, that I'd somehow held on to the reins.

"Take more care, Mike," said Mr. Butler, but he didn't seem to realize that the action had been deliberate, and the ride started off again while I was still struggling to get my foot into the stirrup. Rosie leaned over and grabbed Tim's headband as I scrambled on.

"He's done it again," she said quietly.

"Yes, and no one even cares," I said bitterly. "I know I haven't said anything, but you'd think they'd have noticed by now that every time something happens to me, Mike's nearby, looking pleased with himself. Well, that's definitely it. I'm going to get back at him today, somehow."

"And he might have hurt Tim," said Rosie. "Poor, poor Tim."

We had a couple of short canters, and I was surprised at how easy and smooth it was – much more comfortable than trotting – but with an edge of danger that just added to the thrill.

111

When we stopped for our picnic, we had to lead the ponies to a particular bit of gravelly riverbank so they could drink, and then tie them up in the shade of a small wood. Mr. Butler warned us only to get near the river at that point, because everywhere else was very boggy. That's when I thought of my plan. It was hot in the sun and most people, including Mike, took off their riding boots. That made things even better. I took Rosie to one side and explained my idea. We had to think of a way of distracting everyone's attention for a few minutes.

"I know, I'll start another argument with Kate," said Rosie. "That won't be hard."

I felt a bit sorry for Kate, who'd been looking rather sad and lonely all morning, but it was an easy solution to our problem. In a few seconds she and Rosie were yelling at each other and everyone else crowded around, waiting to see if they'd start fighting again. Mr. Butler and Caroline had been sitting some way off and came over to see what was going on. As soon as everyone was busy, I untied Bilbo's halter rope and ran with him to the far side of the trees. He trotted next to me quite happily, though I made sure I was holding him well away from me – I hadn't forgotten his tendency to bite. The river was quite shallow there and the ground perfectly firm. Better and better. We were hidden in the trees, but I could still hear shouting and laughter and Mr. Butler's stern voice. I crossed the river carefully, the water splashing halfway up my boots, and gave Bilbo's flank a hefty slap. He whinnied in surprise, and set off exactly as I'd hoped, along the riverbank but on the opposite side. I ran back to the others as fast as I could, slowing down as I got near, and still no one had noticed me, except Chris. I winked at him hard, hoping that he wouldn't say anything, and he looked puzzled but stayed quiet.

Then Rosie, seeing me back, let things subside. Kate was

looking livid but once Rosie refused to argue, she couldn't do more than sulk. Within a few moments, the crowd surrounding them had turned away.

Then Adam said, "Isn't that Bilbo on the other side of the river, Mike?"

Everyone looked.

"You idiot!" said Mr. Butler. "Didn't I tell you to tie your ponies up carefully? He could get stuck in the bog and lame himself over there. Go and get him – get a move on!"

Hurriedly, Mike put his boots on, then set off at a run. To my disappointment, he managed to jump across the river by stepping on stones that jetted out of the river. If he got Bilbo back without any trouble, our revenge would be wasted.

But then he took a step onto green grass and it wasn't – it was deep, oozing bog. His leg disappeared up to his knee and he tugged it back out with both hands.

"Come back, Mike, you'll get stuck!" shouted Mr. Butler.

Mike started to turn, but both feet sank at once and he lost his balance. He flailed wildly for a long moment, his arms waving and his face furious, and then he was sprawled full-length on the soggy, squelchy ground.

"Get up!" someone yelled.

He tried to, but every time he got halfway, his weight would make him sink, he'd lose balance, and he'd fall again. By now, everyone except Mr. Butler – even Caroline – was in fits of laughter. He looked so funny, like a filthy scarecrow, getting up and slipping over again and again.

We were weak with laughter when he finally got himself onto both feet, facing us. He was just getting his balance right to step back into the stream and cross over when Bilbo, who had been watching his antics with curiosity, decided to join in. Delicately placing his hoofs onto the tufts of solid turf that interspersed the bog, he walked up to his rider, and,

perhaps in a spirit of helpfulness, nipped his shoulder gently. Completely taken by surprise, Mike toppled forward one last time, this time right into the stream, and this time even Mr. Butler had to laugh.

In the end, Mr. Butler had to wade across to Mike and haul him up. Caroline crossed in the woods and managed to catch Bilbo without getting herself – or him – too messy. Mike, though, was covered from head to foot with slimy mud – much worse than I'd been after the muckheap incident. He stood, dripping, in front of Mr. Butler, red with embarrassment and anger, rubbing his shoulder.

"This is the last straw," said Mr. Butler, none too pleased himself now he'd stopped laughing. "Having one group of riders soaking wet during the day is one thing, but for it to happen a second time... How did Bilbo get over to the other side of the stream? I've told you all till I'm blue in the face to tie the ponies up properly."

I watched Mike steadily, though I could feel a guilty blush licking my cheeks. Rosie met his glare squarely, too. Chris glanced across at me, just for a moment, and Mike immediately caught on and looked daggers at me. I forgot all about our plan that Mike should know I'd set him up. A shiver ran down my spine. Had I just done something really foolish?

Caroline was told to take the glowering Mike home. Rosie gave me a big hug as we went to get our ponies.

"Don't worry," she said. "I bet what I said is true, that he'll stop bullying you now."

I wasn't so sure but at least Mike was safely out of the way. I stroked Tim's soft nose. He whiffled softly into my fingers, and I decided to concentrate on the present and leave the future to sort itself out.

After all the excitement, we mounted and set off. Rachel showed me how to do something called "Round the World in

115

80 Days". You have to take your feet out of the stirrups, hold the reins just in one hand, and then lift one leg over the pony's back till you're sitting sideways in the saddle. Then you carry on with the other leg, so you're facing the back, and then finally you swivel around to the front again, swapping hands on the reins as you go. Rachel did it very smoothly but when I tried it wasn't so easy, especially as the ground was quite rough so Tim was being bumpy. The worst moment was coming around to the second side – my bottom skidded on the saddle, and I thought I'd slip off. But I jiggled back into the saddle and quickly got my right leg over the pommel so that I was facing the front again. Tim didn't seem to mind – I'm not sure he even noticed – and we carried on with a few other tricks, easier things like leaning back in the saddle till you're lying down, only with your feet still in the stirrups, and also knotting the reins together so they won't trip the pony up and folding your arms or sticking them out sideways so as to practice balance. All the riders except Mr. Butler joined in and it was a real laugh, especially when we tried to do synchronized "Round the World" turning, like synchronized swimming, which worked brilliantly, except that Chris kept pretending to nearly fall off which got a bit tedious.

After a while we reached an area where some tree felling had been taking place, and Mr. Butler told us to dismount and give the ponies a rest.

He sorted us so that one rider was holding two or three ponies, and set the others to collect smooth branches and lay them at intervals along the track, to create a line of low jumps. Although I'd coped OK with the cantering, I felt really nervous, and could barely hang on to Tim and Twinkle while I waited.

Mr. Butler explained what to do.

"Those of you who've never jumped," he began, "you

don't have to start now! Just walk or trot your pony along the track and let him step over the obstacles. You'll hardly notice a thing. Give him a little more rein than usual and lean forward."

I heaved a sigh of relief. Mr. Butler grinned at me. "Thought you were going to have to do it at a gallop?" he asked. "You'll have to come here another time and then we'll see." I murmured an embarrassed reply, but inside I vowed I'd be back, next year or before, and that I'd be doing as much as anyone then.

"If you know what you're doing," went on Mr. Butler, "have a try over the jumps at a trot first. Then, if you like, try at a canter, but be careful."

"These aren't proper jumps anyway," said Chris. "I'm used to proper fences, not poles on the ground."

"I'm sure you are," Mr. Butler said patiently, "but there's a difference between riding in a field with lightweight poles on blocks and riding down a rough track over fallen boughs, and that's what we're doing. OK?"

"Easy-peasy," said Kate airily.

A good half of the group opted to walk or trot their ponies over the branches. It was an odd sensation, but not at all alarming, and I half-wished I dared to go faster. Then we watched the others.

They came down the line one after the other. Phil came first, at a neat, controlled canter. Rachel also cantered down easily, but Kate, who was next, couldn't persuade her pony to go over any of the boughs. She sat kicking him helplessly, tears in her eyes. Mr. Butler gave her a riding crop. She turned her pony back a few feet, then wheeled round and approached the first pole. As she got near, she gave the pony a tap on the neck, but it made no difference. He refused. Kate was bright red, especially as Rosie, who'd trotted down with me, was watching with a broad grin on her face.

117

"Don't let him get away with it – give him a good hard whack!" called Mr. Butler.

She tried again, and this time the pony tittupped over half-heartedly, and completed the rest of the course at a walk.

"Bad luck," said Caroline.

"Bad riding, you mean," commented Rosie to me, judging her voice carefully so Kate would overhear. Kate glared at her and joined the furthest point of the line.

Chris was next and couldn't resist the temptation to show off. He'd broken off a bendy stick and used it to hit Poppy hard. She set off at a fast canter, cleared the first two branches in a flurry of hooves, and then stopped dead in front of the next. Taken by surprise, Chris, who'd been leaning well forward, swung around her neck, dangled absurdly for a moment, and then squelched down onto a particularly muddy patch of ground.

There were hoots of laughter from everyone, including Mr. Butler, as Chris clambered back on to Poppy, plastered with sticky mud and gooey leaves.

"You won't have another try until you give me that stick," said Mr. Butler. "That's a good, brave pony, and it was your fault she refused; you went at it too fast and she couldn't take off in time."

Chris threw the stick to the ground and rode back to the start. He kicked into a trot and cleared the first two branches again. As he approached the third, he kicked hard, but the pony swerved suddenly sideways and stopped. Again he was propelled forward, this time right over her head. As he landed, he tucked his head under and did a sort of head over heels turn, ending up flat on his back in the mud again.

There was a moment's pause as everyone waited to see how he would take it, especially after what had happened to Mike a couple of hours earlier, but when he stood up, there

118

was a big smile on his face and he joined in the laughter that followed.

He's really quite brave, I thought. It can't be easy making a fool of yourself and not seeming to mind. I bet he does really. And my thoughts added, inconsequentially, I hope my Tim grows up to be a bit like that.

Chapter 12

Mike was leaning on the farm gate waiting for us. He looked moody and scowled at me, but Rosie stuck close by me all evening. There wasn't anything special organized, but the boys played football for ages. Jane and Kate joined in, though Ed was still pointedly ignoring Kate; Rachel, Rosie, and me had a cozy time gossiping drinking cocoa and eating cookies.

There was something on my mind, though. The leggings Mom bought me for riding had been a good substitute for jodhpurs so far. The time they got filthy and soaked, Mrs. Butler had them clean and dry by morning, and the rest of the time they were close enough to the real thing, so no one had mentioned them. I was wearing rain boots instead of proper riding boots or short jodhpur boots, of course, but so were Jane and Matthew.

But the continual pressure of the saddle had worn the cheap material away. There was a series of gaping holes all along the inside seams and, even if I got a hold of some needle and thread and mended them, they would never hold together for another day. I could always wear jeans, of course, but Mr. Butler was obsessive about not wearing jeans. "Uncomfortable, impractical in rain, definitely not riding wear," he had said.

I bundled the leggings into the bottom of the wardrobe

and got into bed, thinking furiously. They were too far gone to mend. What else could I do? I could try putting the leggings over jeans to disguise them. Maybe I could "borrow" someone else's jodhpurs. Or I could be ill. Or what about pretending to be desperately homesick so I could go home a day early? Nothing seemed very practical, and the last idea actually made me feel homesick for the first time that day. Lying in bed, my brain whirled with visions of being laughed at tomorrow in jeans, especially by Mike, and just to make things worse, with pictures of the twins at home with Mom and Dad, all having a wonderful time without me.

Next morning, the sun was shining brilliantly. Rosie pulled the covers off me and laughed when I moaned.

"Come on, it's a fantastic day and it's our last proper one, so don't be lazy! Let's get outside and see the ponies before anyone else does."

She was already dressed. Kate was fast asleep. I looked at my watch – 6 a.m. The twins will be standing up in their cribs by now, I thought, yelling for food and company. It'll be nice to be there with them the day after tomorrow.

Rosie gave me a friendly punch. "Come on!" she urged. "Or I'll go without you!"

"Coming." I scrambled into my clothes quickly. By the back door there was a sort of lobby where everyone left their boots. I carefully wrapped the flared bottoms of my jeans round my ankles and pushed my feet into my rain boots. Rosie was tugging at her riding boots and getting all hot and bothered.

"I wish Mom hadn't gone and bought us these," she grumbled. "They're supposed to be better when you're riding, but they're awful to get on or off. You're lucky having those rain boots."

"You've got proper jodhpurs, though," I said enviously.

"What? Oh, yeah, they're great. We had to wear tracksuit

121

trousers before. But you've been wearing sort of jodhpurs, haven't you?"

"Not really. They're just leggings, but they've fallen apart. Oh Rosie, I'm really worried about today. I've only got these jeans and you know what Mr. Butler says about people wearing them. I'm sure he'll yell at me and then everyone will think I'm poor and stupid and everything."

Rosie stopped pulling at her boot and looked at me seriously. "Well, if you haven't got anything else, you'll just have to wear your jeans. I'd lend you something but I've only got jeans and jodhpurs with me, and Kate's the same. But I bet if you explained to Mr. Butler, he'd understand. He goes on and on about things but I don't think he means to upset people. D'you want me to talk to him about it?"

"D'you think that would help?"

"Probably not. Why don't you just wait and see what happens? He might not even notice."

"Maybe. Thanks, Rosie. It's – it's not Mom and Dad's fault they can't afford to get me everything – "

"Do stop moaning about money. Anyone would think you were the only person here who doesn't come from a super-rich family. If we had lots of money, we'd all own ponies for a start. Anyway, what our parents have doesn't make us any better or worse. We're just us."

Rosie said it with such conviction, that I kept my mouth closed. It was a perfect day. Little white clouds were drifting gently across the pale blue sky, and the same breeze that moved them was making the daffodils dance. The grass in the paddock sparkled in the early morning light, and there was that lovely, fresh, open-air scent that I'd smelled when I arrived but had almost stopped noticing over the last few days. We sat together on the paddock railings, our feet dangling, chewing long stalks of sweet grass, and watching the grazing ponies. I called "Tim!" experimentally and I was so thrilled when he lifted his head from the grass, saw me, and trotted across. He buried his soft muzzle in my tummy while I stroked his nose.

"I'm going to miss you," I told him sadly. "I have to go home tomorrow."

"So do we all," said Rosie practically, "but he'll still be here if you come back. Will you?"

"Oh yes."

"Even with all the trouble you've had with Mike?"

"He can't do much to me in one day," I said. "And whatever happens now, I'll never forget seeing him flat on his face in all that mud."

Rosie giggled. "They say revenge is sweet. Do you want to do anything else if we get the chance?"

"Why bother?" Tim put his head down to crop the grass at our feet, and I stretched my arms in the warm air, feeling the sun on my back. "You were right just now, about me being too sensitive. But I have done one thing this week, I've found out how to deal with people – like Mike bullying me. There's no point getting all flustered. I've done my best to get equal and now I'll just get on with my life. If he wants to be friends, then I'll see. Otherwise, I don't care."

Rosie stared at me. "Wow," she said. "You sound like a grown-up. Go on, give me the benefit of your great mind. What d'you think of Phil?"

I looked sideways at her. Rosie seemed quite serious, not making fun of me. "Underneath all that whining he's OK," I said, "but he's spoiled, being the only one. I know what that's like, a bit. And he's never found out the fun of having brothers or sisters, so he's no good at coping with the rest of us." I laughed, embarrassed. "At any rate, that's my theory. I wouldn't take any notice if I were you."

Rosie laughed too. "OK," she agreed. "Of course, you know he likes you, don't you?"

123

"Do you think he does? I couldn't figure out if that's what it was or not. I haven't had a boyfriend. Have you?"

"I wouldn't want one. Look at the mess it's got Kate into." She paused. I slid off the fence and picked a handful of grass from outside the paddock, where it grew thick and juicy, and held it out to Tim. I haven't told you what that feels like, have I? It's quite scary at first; ponies have massive teeth and there doesn't seem any reason why they shouldn't eat your fingers too. But instead they sort of whiffle the grass away and then stand munching with a great moustache of grass sticking out either side of their mouths.

"Why don't we go wandering around the fields and then see if there's any breakfast yet?" I suggested.

We crossed through the paddock past the bunching, jostling ponies. The next two fields belonged to the farm and had been allowed to go wild. We meandered contentedly among the long grasses starred with flowers, enjoying each other's company without needing to talk.

When we were nearly back at the farmhouse, Rosie said, "I'll tell you something about you, now, if you like."

"What?"

"When you got here, I think you were scared stiff, not so much of the riding but of all of us, weren't you?"

"I was terrified."

"Well, you've changed."

We were back in the yard now, and some of the boys were emerging, bleary-eyed and yawning, from the cottage next to the farmhouse where their bedrooms were, so we didn't say any more. But while I was having breakfast, and later getting Tim ready for the ride, I thought about what Rosie had said. I don't mind about the twins any more, I thought, and I've coped OK with Mike and Phil, and I'm doing all right with the riding, so all I'm really worried about is these silly jeans. So what – it's not going to rain today, and if Mr.

124

Butler says anything I'll just have to tell him I don't have anything else to wear. He's hardly going to stop me riding, after all.

I finished tacking up Tim, checked his feet, and swung up into the saddle. As I leaned over to adjust his girth it hit me just how much I'd learned about ponies. Rosie on Twinkle grinned happily at me as I kicked Tim to the yard entrance so I'd be one of the first out. We walked the ponies along the lane in the bright sun. I could control Tim quite well, especially when cars went by, and he hardly ever tried to put his head down to the grass verge any more. Then we turned onto a track and Mr. Butler told us to trot on. Trotting and walking in turn, we went through dappled woods for a good hour, gradually climbing higher. I could see why Mr. Butler disapproved of jeans – they were really uncomfortable where the seams rubbed my thighs and a bit too tight after all the food I'd eaten, and the bundle of material round my ankles hurt, too – but everything else was so perfect I could ignore that.

At last, there was bright light ahead, and we emerged, blinking, on to a wide hilltop, with the most amazing views in every direction. Even the boys, who usually claimed to be bored by things like that, were silenced. We dismounted to give the ponies a rest after the long uphill haul, and Caroline gave out chocolate biscuits. We wandered about contentedly, chatting in small groups, while the ponies snatched a snack of fragrant grass. Phil was the only person who stood alone, his back to the others. I nudged Rosie and pointed to him. We went over and said hello. He'd stuffed his mouth so full of chocolate that he looked like a hamster, but he managed a muffled "Hi."

"Would you like some more?" I asked. I felt sorry for him. "You didn't eat much breakfast, did you? I had loads; I'm still full."

Phil grabbed the chocolate.

"If there are teams for the gymkhana this afternoon, do you want to be together?" he said directly to me, very obviously ignoring Rosie.

"Well..." I said awkwardly, "I don't really know ... There's Rosie, you see."

"Go on," he urged, swallowing hard and biting off another chunk of chocolate. "She'll want to be with Kate, now she and Ed have broken up." He sounded pleased.

Rosie raised her eyebrows. "Do you know what – you're a greedy pig," she stated baldly. "I can't imagine why Jess stands up for you. You're almost as bad as my sister."

"Oh now don't start with Kate," I pleaded. "You hardly mentioned her this morning when we were discussing everyone. I thought you'd stopped letting her upset you."

"Just kept busy complaining about me, instead, I suppose?" said Phil in a nasty voice. "Typical girls, interfering busybodies."

"Phil! We didn't! And I've just given you all that chocolate!"

"Leave him alone," advised Rosie. "He's happier being miserable. One day he'll grow up." She shot a hard glance at Phil. "Let's go and check the ponies."

We left Phil looking confused and angry.

"I wish I'd never said anything," I said sadly, as we stroked Tim and Twinkle. "Maybe if..."

"I said this morning you'd changed," said Rosie, "but you're still hoping to sort out everyone's lives. You can't, you know. And me and Kate – we've been dealing with each other all our lives; we know each other. It's not your job to sort us out."

"I suppose not."

I felt deflated and disappointed but there wasn't time to brood. The minute we started again we went straight into cantering along the wide grassy hilltop and though I was still a bit scared it was much easier than I'd expected. So long as I didn't think about falling off, it was like flying with the wind rushing through my hair and the steady pounding of Tim's hooves muffled against the soft grass. The worst part was stopping, because that's when I felt most wobbly, but nothing awful happened, and Caroline, who'd stayed comfortingly close to me all the time, said I'd done really well. And then we had a fast trot back along lanes back to the farm with Mr. Butler and Caroline riding along the column warning everyone that we could expect some very hard work before we'd get any food.

They were right, of course. We had to take all the tack off the ponies, groom them forever, turn them out into the paddock, and then polish the saddles and bridles. It was rough even though we'd done all that tack cleaning earlier in the week. Mr. Butler inspected the ponies and told Chris, Rachel, and Adam that their grooming wasn't good enough. They had to catch their ponies, and have another try. Meanwhile, he examined the tack with an eagle eye and told several people to do bits again. As he came towards me, I was positive he was going to say something about my jeans, but all he said was, "Not bad, Jessica. Just give the headband a bit more elbow grease and then you can go in for lunch."

I rubbed till the leather all shone, and then hung up the tack and went indoors. There was hot soup and piles of sandwiches. Gradually the room filled up as everyone finished and was allowed to go in for lunch. Even Phil ate a couple of sandwiches, though he sighed dramatically over them as if he was hoping for sympathy. Not me, I thought. All he wants is someone to be sorry for him, and I don't see why I should be. I do wish I could do something about Rosie and Kate, though, I thought, watching them glaring at each other from different ends of the room. I like Kate and Rosie's my best

127

friend here. I wish I could think of a way to get them to like each other again.

Mr. Butler came in.

"OK, everyone," he said, "this is your last session." There was a chorus of groans. "So, to finish the week off in style, this afternoon is gymkhana time. While you've been guzzling your lunch, we've been getting things ready. Whiz out there, tack up, and we'll start in 10 minutes."

There was a stampede towards the door. The ponies were quickly caught again, looking distinctly puzzled, as usually, once they were turned out into the paddock, that was the end of their day. Gleaming from their grooming, and wearing equally shining saddles and bridles, they were soon lined up along the paddock fence.

The first game was bending. Mr. Butler had put 10 milk crates in two lines the length of the field and, two at a time, we had to race in and out of the crates, turn at the end, and race back. I was against Phil, and he cantered Bramble neatly up and down while I was still persuading Tim to trot, now he wasn't following any other ponies. I trailed back to the start feeling rather silly, but there was no time to sulk. Another heat was already beginning. The six winners were paired off and raced again, which left three leaders – Chris, Phil, and Rachel.

"How are you going to work out the overall winner?" asked Ed.

"They can each race the other one – that'll be three races – and then we'll see if there's a winner," said Mr. Butler.

Chris went first against Phil, but he didn't have a chance as Bramble was much bigger than Poppy so he covered the ground far faster. Then Phil raced Rachel. Their ponies were much the same size but Rachel guided Star so neatly around the obstacles that she won by a whisker.

"One all to Phil and Rachel," said Rosie. "Come on,

Rachel!" But Rachel and Star were both very excited. When the whistle went, she lost all control of him, and he galloped to the far end of the paddock. Meanwhile, Chris was carefully negotiating the blocks and cantering back to the start.

"A draw," announced Mr. Butler. "Two points each."

Mrs. Butler, who'd spent most of the week indoors preparing our enormous meals, had for once come outside and was in charge of a large scoreboard propped up against the tack room door.

There was a potato race next. There were four buckets at one end of the paddock, and a bag of potatoes at the other. You had to grab a potato, mount, and gallop to the other end, drop it in the bucket without getting off your pony, and ride back for the next potato, until the time was up. The first heat was won by Rosie, and the second by Ed. I was in the last heat, riding against Kate, Chris, and Jane, and I didn't think I had a chance. But when it came to it, I kicked Tim into a canter without even realizing, and tore up and down the paddock six times while the others only managed four or five.

"Well done," said Mr. Butler, laughing. "Greased lightning, eh? You missed with two of the potatoes, but so did the others, so you're in the finals."

I was determined not to let Tim get carried away in the final like Rachel's pony had. I kept him on a tight rein and was very careful to throw the potatoes accurately. I was concentrating so hard, I didn't even notice how the other two were doing and was surprised when the whistle blew. I'd only got three potatoes this time; Ed had four and Rosie had somehow managed seven! So I only got one point while the others had two or three, but I didn't mind – at least there was something up against my name.

"OK, everyone," said Mr. Butler. "The last race before a short break is the dressing-up race."

I thought that sounded fun, but the older riders didn't look too excited.

"Do we have to?" pleaded Rob. "It's a bit juvenile."

"You're enough to scare any pony, even without stupid clothes," commented Matthew cheekily. Rob threw himself onto him and there was a short interlude while they tussled on the ground.

"Break it up!" called out Mr. Butler wearily. The two boys got up, grinning.

I heard someone say, "Silly pair of babies." It was Kate who'd been very quiet all day.

"Boys will be boys, my Mom says," I said, thinking this would be a good moment to be friendly.

"Are girls any better? My sister's not." Kate flounced off. I shrugged in despair, and felt annoyed when I saw Phil watching.

Meanwhile, Adam and Jane had been laying out piles of clothes the length of the paddock. There were clownlike baggy trousers, bright checked shirts, ancient jackets, cardigans, and the most peculiar hats.

"Where on earth does all this come from?" asked Jane, examining a purple picture hat adorned with green feathers and pale blue netting.

"Not our cast-offs, you'll be glad to know," said Mr. Butler with a chuckle. "We get most of them from yard sales, ready for when we get groups like you."

"Will there be another group next week?" asked Rachel.

"Oh yes. Of course. It's only during the holidays that we run these sort of groups."

"Which do you like better?" asked Ed.

"A group like you can be very hard work," said Mr. Butler with feeling. "But overall we enjoy the mixed groups. It's interesting watching you all settle down and make friends and all that."

"You sound like a scientist with us as the experiment," said Chris.

"No, it's the poor ponies who're the experiment," said Caroline, joining us. "Week in, week out, they have different riders. No wonder they enjoy their Sundays off!"

I thought of Tim, being ridden by someone else next week, and someone else the week after, and a lump came into my throat.

"If someone comes back," I said, "can they have the same pony as before?"

"Usually," said Mr. Butler. He added with a smile, "We'll keep Tim for you, don't fret."

We lined up for the dressing-up race. There were three lots of clothes, so there'd be four heats. Then there'd be semi-finals, and then the final.

Chris won the first heat. He was small and agile, so he could slip the clothes on quickly and easily while his opponents were still stuck with one leg in a pair of trousers. He came storming down to the start, Poppy's legs flashing, and then boasted to everyone how easy it was to win.

The next group were all boys and all equally bad at the race. It was hysterical watching them floundering about with both arms stuck down one sleeve, or a hat shifted back to front over their eyes, desperately trying to get back onto their excited ponies. Mike won, though he wasn't really wearing the clothes – they sort of hung off him. The next wave was all girls – Rosie, me, and Kate. Mike trotted past us at the starting line, aimed a kick at me and made a rude face, but I didn't let myself react. We set off in a bunch but as I slid off Tim by the trouser pile, Kate had already got on her trousers and was on to the shirt. I got my boot caught in a trouser leg, and had a terrible job pulling it out, especially as Tim kept trying to follow Magpie, so I was forced to hop after him. Rosie, meanwhile, got stuck with the trousers halfway up her legs. In the end she gave up the struggle to pull them either off or on and flung herself sideways across the saddle. Unfortunately, this confused Twinkle, who trotted off in the wrong direction while Rosie hung on desperately. There were shouts of laughter from the spectators as Mr. Butler carefully turned Twinkle back towards the race and slapped her flank. She broke into a fast trot, and Rosie slid clumsily down the side of the saddle and landed on the ground with a hefty thump.

Everyone was so busy laughing at Rosie, that no one noticed Kate had completed the race and won, her face like thunder. I was still trying to put on a cardigan with so many holes it was more like grubby lace, so I dropped it and led Tim back to the start. Kate looked venomously at Rosie, furious with her for stealing her glory.

Jane won the fourth heat easily; while Ed and Adam were still tied up with trousers, she sailed through the whole course.

They played off two against two, Chris versus Mike and Kate versus Jane. I wondered if the old rivalry between the two boys would make a difference. Certainly Mike looked really determined, and though his dressing-up was a bit sketchy, he won easily. Jane and Kate seemed to be in unison, arriving at each pile of clothes at the exact same instant, and it was only at the very last moment that Jane's pony thrust forward and reached the line.

The two finalists got ready to go again. Everyone crowded around, encouraging their favorite. Once all the clothes were ready again, Mr. Butler shouted "Go!" and they were off.

"Mi-ike, Mi-ike, Mi-ike!" came a chant from his friends that took me straight back to that first day when Ed and Kate got together and Mike dared Chris to ride Captain. I clenched my fists and yelled encouragement to Jane in the loudest voice I could manage.

By now, the ponies, normally very placid, had been infected by the excitement, and leapt into action enthusiastically. Jane's pony was very neat-footed and halted by the trousers easily. Mike's bigger pony, Bilbo, overshot and had to be hauled back round, losing him valuable seconds, but he had easier trousers to put on and was back in the saddle and galloping off while Jane was still pulling on hers. He grabbed a shirt and flung it round his neck, vaulted back onto Bilbo, and kicked on.

"Come back, Mike! You have to put it on!" yelled Mr. Butler, but everyone was shouting so loudly Mike couldn't hear. He added a jacket to the shirt round his shoulders, cantered to the hats, and was back at the start with a broad grin on his face while Jane was still putting on her cardigan.

"You have to wear the clothes!" shouted Mr. Butler again. Mike suddenly heard. His face, half-hidden by a disintegrating straw hat, went bright red.

"Can I go back?" he shouted.

"Yes, but get a move on!"

Mike pulled Bilbo round and tore back up the line – but it was too late. Jane had quietly collected and put on all the clothes, and was trotting calmly to the finish.

She was quickly surrounded by an excited, cheering crowd. Mike threw his dressing-up clothes to the ground angrily and stood by his pony. Everyone ignored him. Mrs. Butler wrote busily on the scoreboard. Chris, Rosie, and Jane each had three points, most of us had two or one, and Matthew, Rob, and Adam didn't have any at all yet.

"Time for a break," announced Mr. Butler. "You'd better tie the ponies to the rail if you haven't already, and a couple of you can take buckets of water over. There's squash and biscuits over in the tack room; we'll start the race again in 15 minutes."

Chapter 13

"Wow, it's already 4 p.m.!" said Rosie to me as we took four biscuits each. "I wonder what else we're doing?"

"Chris asked for a treasure hunt," I reminded her. "There are always treasure hunts in pony books – I've always wanted to do one."

We sat on a straw bale, our backs against the warm wood of the tack room wall, and the sun blazing down.

"It's boiling for April," I remarked, taking off my sweatshirt. "Won't it be horrible to be back in our towns tomorrow?"

"Don't even think about it," said Rosie with a shudder. "I'm going to save every penny of pocket money and do jobs for anyone who'll let me so I can come back in October."

"Me too. Should we call each other and see how we're doing?"

"Of course. Maybe you could come and stay in the summer."

We slumped comfortably, propped against each other, and had almost dozed off when Mr. Butler's voice roused us.

"OK, now for the final event – the treasure hunt," he said. "And the most important thing is that you're not to leave our land; I don't want anyone straying onto the road. But you can go into the paddock and the fields beyond, and into the stable yard, and into the little wood over there. And you're to go on horseback whenever you can, but if you get off to collect something, one of the pair holds both the ponies."

"We're going in pairs then?" asked Rosie, sticking close to me.

"Yes, but you draw your partners from the hat."

Mr. Butler held out one of the dressing-up hats, which was filled with screwed up pieces of paper. Rosie made a face at me and picked one.

"Oh no!" she shrieked in mock horror. "I've got Ed!" Everyone laughed, except Ed.

I held back. It'd be just my luck to get Phil and have to put up with his moaning, but Jane picked Phil.

Mike put his hand in the hat. "Jess," he announced flatly. "Wow, aren't I lucky?"

Rob and Adam sniggered. Rosie squeezed my arm. My stomach took a quick ride to the ground and stayed there.

The next pairs were Chris and Adam and then Matthew and Rob.

"That leaves Rachel and Kate. OK, off you go," said Mr. Butler. "Here are your clues. You've got an hour to collect everything."

He handed each pair a typewritten list.

A feather
Five different wild flowers
A red stone
Some sheep's wool
An eggshell (no stealing from nests)
Some moss
A nut
A length of binder twine

Mike and me stood way apart. I craned over to see the list without actually getting nearer. The other pairs consulted, jumped onto ponies, and dispersed round the farm till only Mike and me were left.

"Aren't you two trying?" asked Mr. Butler cheerfully, pouring charcoal onto the massive barbecue. "Your time'll be up before you start at this rate."

"Oh, come on," said Mike grudgingly, stuffing the list into his pocket. "I suppose even you can hold the ponies while I do the work."

I bit my lip to stop myself from retorting and got up on Tim. It's not fair, I thought, that my very last ride on Tim should be spoiled by having to be with Mike. I followed him as he trotted across the yard into the paddock, and drew rein next to him by the far fence.

"Well, get off then," he snapped.

"What are we looking for?"

"A feather. You'd better hold the ponies."

I sighed and held Tim and Bilbo while Mike searched the grass for a feather. At least the ponies liked each other and nuzzled each other companionably – Bilbo liked nipping other ponies, but today he seemed chilled. After a bit I coughed.

"If you let me see the list, I could be thinking about the other things we've got to get."

"If you want." Mike tossed the paper across. Trying to catch it while holding two halter ropes was too difficult and the list floated to the ground.

"Stupid girl!" Mike remarked scathingly. "It'll probably be too wet to read now."

I'd had enough. "Don't be ridiculous!" I flared up. "The grass is bone dry – we've been sitting on it all day. And I'm just as capable of finding these things as you are – if not better. OK?"

Stuffing the list into my jeans pocket, I pulled the ponies to the corner of the paddock where some trees grew. In their shade, several feathers gleamed, and I picked one up and waved it at Mike triumphantly.

"What's next on the list?" asked Mike, carefully avoiding my eyes.

"Five wild flowers," I read. "Well, I can see three different ones without even trying." I pushed Bilbo away before he ate them and picked the three – one blue and two yellow – don't ask me what they were called. Mike sneered as if he thought noticing flowers was truly pathetic, but I ignored him and gave him the reins. I found a daisy growing in the middle of the paddock and there was a dandelion in flower nearby.

"Not bad," said Mike, a shade less unpleasantly. "Next?"

I looked again. "A red stone. That should be easy."

But it wasn't. We looked everywhere, in the paddock, on the graveled drive, around the stable yard, and all the stones were gray or white or brown. Mike looked at his watch.

"We're wasting time," he said. "Think. Where have you seen a red stone this week?"

"Nowhere," I said. "It's not the sort of thing you see. Except...follow me!"

I grabbed Tim and was up and off in seconds, leaving Mike to scramble on and come after me the best he could. Outside the house, I slithered off and waited impatiently for him to catch up, to give him the reins.

"I've got a hair grip with a red stone," I panted. "That should be OK, shouldn't it?"

"Don't see why not. Go on, get a move on."

I ran into the house, up the stairs and into our room. Yes, the hair grip was by my hairbrush. I put it carefully in a tissue for safety before putting it in my pocket and running outside again.

"What's next?" I gasped, getting up on Tim.

"Sheep's wool. I know – over at the far field, there's some

138

barbed wire and sheep in the next field. They always leave bits of their wool on the fence."

We trotted through the yard and then broke into a canter across the paddock. I felt exhilarated and unsafe all at once, and was glad when we skidded to a halt. Mike thrust his reins into my hands and worked his way along the wire.

"The others got here first," he said gloomily. "I saw Phil just now with a great hefty lump of the stuff – he could've left some for us."

"Let's go on to the next thing and come back to the wool later," I suggested. "Maybe we'll see some as we look for something else."

"What we really ought to do is to look for everything at once," said Mike suddenly. "What else is there?"

"An eggshell, some moss, a nut, some binder twine, and the wool," I said. "Any ideas?"

"Well, there's a nest or two in the hedge by the lane," said Mike. "Maybe there'll be a smashed egg along there, too. It's the right time of year to find them."

We crossed the field, and I held the ponies while Mike looked. Other pairs had had the same idea. There was an excited shriek when Rachel found an empty half of a blackbird's egg, and for ages and ages we all scoured the same area for the other half, but no one else had any luck.

"How are you doing?" Rosie rode up with Ed and stood next to me holding his pony's reins while he searched.

"Not bad, we've got a few things. What about you?"

"I meant, with Mike?"

"Oh. Yeah, I see what you mean. OK, I think."

"Ed's really cool. I can see now why Kate likes him so much," said Rosie. "And he's got some wicked ideas for finding stuff. I bet we win."

Just then Mike came back and vaulted on to Bilbo. "Come on!" he said. "You don't talk to the opposition. Let's go!"

139

Tim and me cantered after him but he soon drew rein, and we stopped next to him.

"Did you get an egg?" I asked eagerly.

"Nope. There aren't any there. Let's look for something else and come back to it later."

I looked at the list. "Binder twine. I don't even know what that is."

"It's that string farmers use. There's always loads of it about when you don't want it." We looked around but everything looked beautifully neat and tidy, with nothing held together with string. Jane and Phil clattered past, looking as if they'd been arguing. It didn't seem a good moment to exchange notes on our finds so far. Then Chris and Adam came around the corner, and Chris had a bundle of blue twine stuffed in his pocket.

"Where did you get that?" called Mike.

"Not a chance," he shouted back.

"Go on, you try," Mike whispered.

What a nerve, I thought, but it did seem a good idea. I walked Tim around a corner and saw Chris and Adam earnestly examining the pebbles in the flowerbeds. No red ones there, I gloated.

"Chris," I hissed. "Over here."

He pulled Poppy's head around and kicked her hard. She skidded into a trot and then as she reached me he reined in sharply, and she halted with a dramatic flourish. Chris was never one to miss out on a chance to show off.

"We're stuck, we can't find any binder twine," I whispered. "Give me a clue? You owe me one..."

I could see that Chris opened his mouth to say no and then thought again.

"Then we're quits, OK?"

I nodded. Boys are so petty sometimes, but if it made him happy and got us what we wanted ...

"Look under those bales of hay at the back of Captain's stable," he hissed, and then he turned Poppy and disappeared with a flurry of hooves.

I trotted Tim back to Mike, and we went together to Captain's stable. We'd been forbidden to go in there as Captain was massive and not particularly friendly. We dismounted and checked to see that no one was lurking about.

"I'll go in if you like," offered Mike.

"Sure," I agreed casually, grabbing Bilbo's reins fast before he could change his mind.

"That's it, boy, just coming past, don't worry about me." Mike's voice sounded unnatural. Captain whinnied, and I could hear him moving restlessly. I dragged the ponies a bit nearer so I could peer in. Mike crouched in the far corner of the stall extricating some blue twine from under a hay bale. As he hurried back to the half-door Captain turned his enormous backside towards him and neighed piercingly.

"Quick, Mike, get out, he's going to kick you!" I yelled.

Mike was over the door in an instant, still holding the twine. Then we both looked in at Captain. He was still in the same position, but somehow any impression of danger had evaporated. Mike raised his eyebrows at me quizzically.

"A bit dramatic, wasn't it?"

"Yeah, well, I thought..."

To my amazement, he smiled. "Thanks, anyway. I wouldn't exactly appreciate getting kicked by those hooves. They're massive."

No one seemed to have heard me screech so luckily no one knew where we'd been, and Mike wasn't making fun of me for panicking. Things were looking up. He stuffed the twine into a pocket and grabbed the list.

"Um...we've still got the egg to find. Got any ideas?"

It suddenly hit me that he wasn't being sarcastic or anything. I thought hard.

141

"I know, we had eggs for breakfast, didn't we? Well, there must be eggshells somewhere in the dustbin."

"Brilliant!" said Mike. "And I'll tell you what, I know where there's some wool, too – I have a sweater my Mom made me bring. Let's go!"

I held the ponies while Mike went to his room. As he came down, he was tying a blue sweater around his waist. "We don't want anyone to guess why I have this," he said with a grin. "Off to the dustbins!"

The side yard where the bins were was very quiet. The shouts and clattering hooves sounded a long way off. I gave Tim's reins to Mike and leaned over into the first bin, rummaging among the debris. Suddenly I was aware that he'd come very close, near enough to easily tip me off-balance into the deep, smelly bin if he wanted to ...

I froze, unable to move a muscle, but nothing happened. Then Mike spoke.

"If there's none in there, I'll try the next one. They really stink, don't they?"

"Ye–es," I said, straightening up and taking the ponies. I took a deep, shivery breath. Here was a chance for a bit more revenge. Casually, I moved up behind Mike as he fished about in the bin. "Almost as bad as that muckheap the other day."

I could tell at once that the arrow had hit its target. Mike leapt upright and turned to face me. He'd gone very white. I clenched my free hand into a fist, ready to punch if he attacked me. For a long moment we just stared at each other.

"OK, fair's fair," said Mike. "I've been pretty mean to you, I suppose. I shouldn't have done all those things. And you didn't really deserve them." He swallowed and looked embarrassed. "You know how it is, with your friends. You have to look good." He hesitated and I just looked at him, letting him do all the work. "I suppose I deserved to get

142

stuck in that bog yesterday," he said. "Do you want to call it quits?"

I gulped. My hand relaxed. "Well, OK," I said slowly. "You started it all, and I've really hated you but maybe we can forget about it and try to be friends."

"I'll try the third bin, then. No pushing in?"

"No pushing in."

Mike delved in the last bin, gave a shout of triumph, and came up with a handful of soggy eggshells. I found an old carrier bag in the first bin to hold them. We grinned at each other and remounted. As the ponies trotted back into the main yard, I said, "Only the moss and the nut to go."

"Moss is easy," said Mike, standing in the stirrups and pulling a huge lump of moss from a hanging basket, which decorated the farmhouse.

"Cool."

The only thing left to find was a nut. We looked at each other blankly.

"There might be some nuts in the wood," Mike said, "but it's the wrong time of year."

"Is it? Anyway, I don't really know what nuts look like, except for the sort of nuts you get at Christmas," I confessed.

"That's what we're talking about," said Mike. "They grow on trees or didn't you know?"

I felt silly. Somehow I had to redeem myself. I thought hard.

"Everyone must be down in the wood now, looking," said Mike gloomily. "That's why there's no one around. It'll be like the wool – we're too late."

That gave me an idea. "But we got the wool by sort of going from a different angle, didn't we? Can't we do the same thing with nuts? Look in the kitchen, or something?"

"That's it! Wicked. Here, I'll hold Tim and you get in there quick."

143

There was no one in the big kitchen. I looked around. There were cupboards everywhere but they all contained plates or saucepans or cleaning stuff, not food. Then I saw a door in the corner and opened it. Inside, there was a whole room lined with shelves and on every shelf there were tins and packets and boxes of all sorts of food. Searching for nuts would take forever. But then I saw a fruitcake on a plate in front of me, and it was decorated with a flower pattern made with almonds! I dislodged one carefully, which made the pattern look odd, so I took another three to make things even, and then I went back out, closing all the doors behind me carefully.

We agreed it was pointless having four nuts so we ate one each and put the other two in the tissue with my hair grip, and then we whizzed to where the Butlers were getting the barbecue ready.

We displayed the treasure proudly. Mr. Butler chuckled as he looked at the nuts. "Well, you're not the first ever to think of using a wool sweater," he said, "but I don't think anyone's thought of raiding the kitchen before and the hair grip's a clever idea, too. Yes, you've got the whole list, and you're first. Well done!"

Mike gave a whoop of joy and bashed me on the back. Tim took exception to this and took me off around the yard, but I gathered the loose reins and got back in control easily enough. A few moments later, Rachel and Kate came tearing into the yard, to be told they were second, followed by Rosie and Ed. As the hour was now up, everyone else soon straggled in, some annoyed and moaning, others laughing and joking.

Everyone waited expectantly for Mr. Butler to announce the overall scores, the only noise from the ponies as they stamped a foot or whinnied.

"OK," he said. "I won't bother with the ones right at the

144

bottom..." someone giggled nervously "...but equal third with three points are Rachel, Kate, Chris, and Ed." There was a murmur as everyone tried to work out who might've done better. It was hard to remember who'd won what after the long afternoon. Kate stuck her tongue out at Rosie. Mr. Butler went on, "Next we have three people sharing second place – Rachel, Rosie, and Jessica." I gave a little shriek. Despite winning the treasure hunt with Mike I hadn't imagined I'd be anywhere in the placings. Rosie squeezed my hand and whispered, "That's upset Kate."

"And finally," said Mr. Butler, "our overall winner, with five points, is – Mike!" There was a big cheer. Mike grinned at everyone and sauntered over to collect his prize, which was a CD gift certificate. We all clapped. Mike gave me a big hug. Phil looked really annoyed, and Rosie's mouth dropped open in amazement.

When the noise died down, Mr. Butler told Kate to fasten the gate from the paddock to the big field beyond. She jumped on to Magpie and cantered off. He told the rest of us to untack the ponies, rub them down, and turn them out into the paddock. "We'll have the barbecue when you're all ready," he said, "so don't take too long." He and Mrs. Butler went indoors.

Weary but cheerful, we started to see to our ponies. Rosie was just asking me to tell her what had happened with Mike when the relaxed atmosphere was broken by a shrill scream.

"It's Kate!" shouted Rosie.

She dropped Twinkle's reins and sprinted to the paddock. We all followed, pulling the ponies with us, or absent-mindedly abandoning them.

Rosie knelt by Kate's still form. Kate's pony was prancing excitedly in the field beyond, his reins dangling between his front feet. Phil managed to catch and calm him, and tied him to the fence.

Kate hadn't stirred. Her face was very white, and she lay awkwardly with one leg skewed at a horrible unnatural angle.

"She's – she's not dead, is she?" someone breathed.

Rosie, chafing Kate's hands between hers and searching her face desperately for consciousness, gave a little moan. "Kate, wake up, please, Kate."

Ed squatted next to her. "Is she breathing?"

Rosie didn't look up but her voice was full of scorn. "Of *course* she's still breathing. Nothing can happen to Kate. Kate, Kate, can you hear me?"

"Stand back a bit, give her some air," ordered Rachel, looking at the rest of us as we crowded round. "Chris, run and get the Butlers – fast!" He shot off. We all stepped back, but we couldn't tear our attention from Kate.

"I heard about someone who was kicked by a horse and was brain-damaged." Ed's voice was strained. "You don't think ...?"

"How do I know? Leave her alone! Don't you know you never move anyone injured?"

Ed drew back a little. Rosie was as white as a sheet, but she went on rubbing her sister's hands. We watched in stunned silence.

Then two things happened. Kate made a small sound, and Mr. Butler pushed through the crowd and dropped on to his knees next to her.

"Don't worry," he said quickly to Rosie, "I won't disturb her, I'll just have a look to see what's wrong." A moment later he heaved a sigh of relief.

"She'll be fine," he announced. "But we'll have to get her to a hospital. She's knocked herself out, and I think she might've broken her leg. Lucky she was wearing her hard hat. OK, she's coming around. Ed, you're quick – run to the house and phone for an ambulance, will you? Tell them where to come."

146

Kate's eyelids were flickering now. She looked around hazily and focused on Rosie's anxious face.

"What happened?"

"You banged your head but you'll be all right," Rosie said gently. "Mr. Butler says have to go to hospital for a check-up. Ed's getting an ambulance."

Kate's hand gripped Rosie's hard.

"You'll come with me, won't you?" she asked.

"'Course I will. Don't be silly, you're my sister." Rosie helped Kate to sit up and hugged her. Kate looked up at Mrs. Butler who'd come to the paddock so suddenly that she was still holding a bag of burger buns.

"My head aches but it's my leg that really hurts," she said.

"You may have broken it. Don't put any weight on it. Wait for the ambulance."

Kate tried to move, but gave a gasp of pain and went even whiter.

"Did you fall off Magpie?" asked Caroline, gently.

"I was trying to close the gate without getting off, like you do," said Kate, struggling not to cry. "Only when I leaned over to get hold of it, Magpie moved and I slipped sideways. My foot got stuck in the stirrup, and that's how I hurt my leg. I landed with an awful crash and then everything went woozy, and then you were all here."

"Just one of those things," said Mr. Butler reassuringly. "You should've been able to manage the gate, but Magpie was probably fidgety after all the races. Never mind. It's the sort of thing that happens to riders sometimes, I'm afraid, no matter how careful or experienced you are. But it really is bad luck."

Rosie, her face pale and drawn, held her sister's hand. Ed ran towards us.

"The ambulance'll be here in about 10 minutes, they said." Blushing deep red, he added awkwardly, "I'm really sorry you're hurt, Kate. And I'm sorry about today...can I do anything?"

"No, it's OK. Rosie'll come with me. You stay with your friends."

Ed looked relieved. Everyone hung around without speaking much until an ambulance turned into the drive. I was a bit disappointed that it wasn't flashing lights or ringing its bell, but I suppose in the depths of the country there's not much traffic to warn. Kate was loaded in carefully, and Mrs. Butler and Rosie went in with her.

"What a week!" said Mr. Butler as the ambulance drove away. He looked around at our serious faces. "Cheer up. She'll be all right – the worst may be a broken leg and that'll mend. Let's try and put it behind us and enjoy the last evening – there's no point worrying about Kate, she's in the best of hands. You'd better finish the ponies, and do Kate's and Rosie's too, and some of you help Caroline with the barbecue and make sure she doesn't eat all the food!"

His cheerful grin was reassuring, and we got on with our jobs. Phil pulled Bramble over to where I was tying Tim to the fence.

"You OK?" he said.

I shrugged. "Suppose so. Poor Kate – and poor Rosie, too."

He took off Bramble's bridle and gazed into the distance while it dripped saliva over his boots. "Sorry if I've been a bit of a pain," he said suddenly. "Look, have this."

He pushed a scrunched up piece of paper in my hand and while I was unscrewing it, led Bramble to the other end of the fence. It was his phone number.

I took my time over Tim, very much aware that this'd be the very last time I'd unsaddle and unbridle him.

"But I'll be out in the paddock first thing tomorrow morning to give you a last grooming," I promised as I worked

148

away with the brush. Tim nuzzled me gently. I stopped for a moment to give him a hug, but he pulled his head away and bent it to nibble at his knee. I patted his soft gray neck and stood back to admire his glossy coat. Then I took his halter rope and led him to the paddock. He pushed past me and cantered friskily onto the grass, kicking his heels up.

Hot tears welled up, and I brushed them away as I watched Tim put his head down to the grass. Rachel led her pony by and I had to move. Someone laughed in the distance. How can anyone be happy now? I leaned on the paddock fence, breathing the sweetly scented air, squinting through the late afternoon sun at the ponies enjoying their weekend rest.

"Food up!" yelled someone. I turned reluctantly to see Caroline and Rachel pushing burgers into buns and handing them out. It was sad Rosie not being there but at least she and Kate were friends again, like sisters ought to be. Maybe even Phil – who was at that very moment picking suspiciously at the edge of his burger – would find out what sharing in a family was about one day. Maybe I'd be able to show him... I thought with sudden pleasure of going home tomorrow to Mom and Dad, to Martha and all my friends, and to Tim and Holly. There'd be so much to tell them about ponies, and people, and ponies again.

"Jess! Come on! Yours is getting cold."

Mike was waving a paper napkin with a bun in it at me.

"Coming!" I called.

But I couldn't leave the paddock, not just yet. I sat on the fence, like I'd done so many times, my eyes so hazy with tears that I couldn't see clearly. A soft bump on my tummy nearly unbalanced me. I rubbed my eyes with the back of my hand and saw that Tim had come back. He'd left his grazing to come to say good-bye.

I hugged his gorgeous, sweet-smelling neck and felt his

150

warm breath against my side. "Bye Tim," I murmured into his ear, knowing that whatever I did tomorrow morning, this was really the end of my pony holiday. "Take care. Enjoy your other riders but wait for me, OK? Because I'll be back – it's a promise."